Fist of the Spider Woman

ARSENAL PULP PRESS | VANCOUVER

Fist of the Spider Woman

Tales of Fear & Queer Desire

edited by AMBER DAWN

ARSENAL PULP PRESS
Suite 200, 341 Water Street
Vancouver, BC
Canada V6B 1B8
arsenalpulp.com

The publisher gratefully acknowledges the support of the Canada Council for the Arts and the British Columbia Arts Council for its publishing program, the Government of Canada through the Book Publishing Industry Development Program, and the Government of British Columbia through the Book Publishing Tax Credit Program for its publishing activities.

"Every Dark Desire" was previously published as Chapter Nine of *Every Dark Desire* by Fiona Zedde (Kensington Publishing, 2007)
An earlier version of "Crabby" appears in *Rent Girls* by Michelle Tea (Last Gasp, 2004)
"Fear of Dying to the Wrong Song" was previously published in *The Clichéist* by Amanda Lamarche (Nightwood Editions, 2005)
An earlier version of "Your Stockholm Syndrome" by Esther Mazakian was previously published in *Event* magazine

Cover illustration by Julie Morstad
Book design by Shyla Seller

Printed and bound in Canada on recycled paper

Library and Archives Canada Cataloguing in Publication:

    Fist of the spider woman : tales of fear & queer desire /
edited by Amber Dawn.

ISBN 978-1-55152-251-7

    1. Horror tales, Canadian (English). 2. Erotic stories, Canadian (English). 3. Lesbianism--Fiction. 4. Canadian fiction (English)--Women authors. 5. Canadian fiction (English)--21st century. I. Dawn, Amber, 1974-

PS8323.L47F48 2009   C813'.0873808353
C2008-907446-7

Thank you

Many thanks to the team at Arsenal Pulp Press—Brian Lam, Robert Ballantyne, Shyla Seller, Janice Beley, Bethanne Grabham, and Susan Safyan—who have, once again, taken a risk in publishing a "risky" book. Thanks also to the cover artist Julie Morstad and to voluntary copy editor Kestrel Barnes.

Contents

Introduction: What Are You Afraid Of?

Amber Dawn

Maybe you remember this happening to you—a renegade coming of age when you realized that being *different* isn't such a bad thing after all, a time when you stopped wishing you fit into the crowd and started building an identity based on standing out from it.

For me, this happened around the time when my grandparents and teachers started referring to me as "young lady." The awkward girl that I had been lifted her shy head and said, "I'm not afraid of you"—meaning curfews, school uniforms, church on Sundays, and any other rules that seemed to exist only to alienate and annoy me. It was then that I discovered a certain power in being different, in breaking the rules.

I kissed my first girl at a chaperoned slumber party, and graffitied my first wall at age twelve (it read "Fuck tha Police" not because my small Southern Ontario town had much of a police presence, but because as a preteen I believed I could truly relate to gangster rap group N.W.A.). I set fires in parking lots, and sucker-punched boys; I also dropped out of Niagara Catholic Secondary and transferred to a vocational high school where I was free to shave off all my hair and wear second-hand lingerie as outerwear. I became a *petite villaine* in my gossipy, close-knit community, a neophyte spider woman with no particular target to seduce or slay. In retrospect, I was just impatient to become the defiantly shameless queer femme I am today.

For many of us, discovering ourselves to be queer or otherwise rebellious women holds some parallels to the shaping of the fictional identities of comic book characters such as Spider Woman, Black Widow, or Gypsy Moth. We put on that "super suit" and thus separate ourselves from the world. But real-life rebellions, even preteen rebellions, don't take place unnoticed. And even though I fancied myself to be fearless, I found out early on that being a woman who sticks out often means being afraid. In high school, there were certain hallways that I avoided for fear of encountering the football team. Years later, I learned there were parts of town where I wouldn't dare to be caught holding hands with another woman. Later still, I realized that certain sex acts made me feel too vulnerable, anxious inside my own body.

These fears aren't mine alone. In fact, "What are you afraid of?" happens to be a standard question among my friends and partners. I suppose we do this as a means of meeting our fears together and to strategize various ways to be safe. Indeed, "safe" is a word frequently used by women: "Call me when you're back safe at home," we might say to one another as we exit the dyke bar, tipsy and wearing our leather boots or low-cut dresses. And creating safety—from staffing rape crisis centres to organizing queer sex parties—largely remains women's work.

But if there is one thing that can be said about rebellious women, it's that we are masterminds at revamping what burdens us, at subverting things to our own advantage. Wallop us with insults—queer, freak, slut, bitch, cunt—and we'll turn them into terms of endearment. Give us yesterday's family dysfunction, and we'll transform it into today's kinky "daddy and little girl" role-play fantasy. As for reclaiming fear, a friend of mine perhaps summed it up best when she told me, "I took Wen-Do women's self-defence classes for years, and the only time I ever use it is to flip my girlfriend onto the bed and pin her down."

I knew long before I began working on this anthology that queer feminine sexuality and fear made good bedfellows, especially when it comes to literature. I've spent many chilling and satisfying nights poring over Sarah Waters, Octavia Butler, and Kathy Acker novels. And I firmly assert that nothing tops off a self-indulgent beach vacation better than a book from the increasingly popular subgenre of lesbian vampire fiction, of which contributor Fiona Zedde is a champion (in "Every Dark Desire," an excerpt from her novel of that name).

In *Fist of the Spider Woman*, fifteen daring authors frankly ask themselves, "What am *I* afraid of?" The aim is not to quell our fears, but to embrace them. In doing so, their work takes on an entirely different form than the familiar thrills of contemporary Hollywood horror films. Perhaps this is not surprising; after all, we are far from the narrowly defined, status quo heterosexuals scared that zombies will invade the suburbs. And let's be honest, if the blinkered characters from most horror films got a good look at what happens inside a radical queer woman's bedroom, they'd be as mortified as if a zombie were running through their neatly manicured back yards. *Fist*'s contributors know what it means to operate outside of the norm. This puts us is in a position to uncover distinctively queer, distinctively woman-centered horrors, and bring life to empathy-worthy victims and villains rarely seen before.

You will not find comic book sidekicks cloned from archetypal male heroes among these pages. Nor will you find the home-wrecking spider woman of *noir* fiction, whose seductive powers only exist to oppose the story's decent and virginal female characters. Of the many versions of this character, perhaps the one that most suits *Fist*'s contributors is a type of matrilineal spider woman as seen in First Nations mythology. This spider woman spins her web to create life, to make connections—her web represents the complex matrix of our relationship to the world and each other. Similarly, *Fist* contributors make connections between fear and desire, power and vulnerability, our internal feelings and external reality.

While all the contributors have honestly earned their title as rebellious women, you'll find their answers to the question "What are you afraid of?" richly diverse. Some have chosen to tackle very real and politically charged horrors, such as Nomy Lamm's tale of a poor, disabled genderqueer whose suspicions of government conspiracies prove to be more than mere paranoia in "Conspiracy of Fuckers," or the hauntingly elusive yet grave portraits of women in war-torn nations seen in the excerpts from Larissa Lai's long poem "Nascent Fashion." Michelle Tea and Amanda Lamarche use humour to trump horror; Tea's "Crabby," a refreshingly multidimensional comic account of surviving pubic lice, reminds us that sexual and personal horrors are often connected, while an unusual phobia is the subject of Lamarche's poem "Fear of Dying to the Wrong Song." Some also treat this anthology as an opportunity to give voice to their darkest, wildest fantasies. Megan Milks' oddly perverted story "Slug" is a perfect example of fear meets fantasy ... and I won't spoil the ghastly and "fowl" ending to Suki Lee's romantic thriller, "Sido."

Instead I will leave you to explore unique—different—fears and desires as revealed by *Fist of the Spider Woman*'s extraordinary contributors.

Slug

Megan Milks

Patty will ask her date to walk her to the door. Patty will play I'm Frightened and Scared to Be Alone in the Deep Dark Night. Of course he will accompany her, despite the drizzle. He will be happy to. Delighted. Then Patty will push him up against the door so he's straddling the doorknob, so it's pressing into his ass crack, and shove his shoulders back, hard, and suck his tongue, hard, and rub his crotch, hard, and push his arms up and over his head and hold them there so that he is her prisoner. It is a good thing she wore her bitch boots tonight. It is a good thing she dressed to be prepared. She will take out her pocket knife and flip up the blade, and she will tickle him with it, slowly, deliberately, while he is still clothed, and she will increase pressure as she moves the knife down from his sternum to his pelvis. His stomach will retract involuntarily. She will press into it more. The flat side of the blade. This is foreplay, pre-foreplay. She will unlock the door, swing it wide, and step back, return to I'm Frightened, and she will squeak, It Looks Like There Could Be a Burglar, Won't You Please Check? I'm So Scared. He will play along, say, It Would Be My Pleasure to Check for the Burglar. Stay Behind Me, Stay Close. And he will grab her wrist firmly and push her behind him, stroking her wrist suggestively. It will be nice.

Patty's date works hard to clear his throat. The first try is phlegmy and meager, a throat-clearing that has miserably failed. He tries again, succeeds, changes the car radio to smooth jazz. Unbearable. Patty uncrosses, then recrosses her legs, begins to clench and unclench her thighs under her plain black skirt.

Patty is a wicked schoolgirl with an SM fetish. Underneath her plain black skirt is a honking big strap-on (Patty makes a mental note: purchase harness and dildo, a formidable dildo). At her command he will get on his hands and knees and enjoy the rug burn, the pathetic motherfucker. Patty is a vicious cunt in bondage gear, with a whip and not afraid to use it, slave. Patty likes to be tied up, chained up with needles through her nipples, getting burned to blood black with cigarettes and branding irons. Patty enjoys biting and being bitten, hard, like a starved vampire. She also enjoys bestiality; triple, quadruple penetration; and feverish, drugged-up sex parties. Sex parties have lots of drugs. What kinds of drugs will Patty's sex party have? Patty is in the middle of being gangbanged, which means violence and overwhelming numbers of cocks at once. Patty is the one with the cock, and she is making him eat it, swallow it, gag.

"You're not giving me much to go on," he says. He has been talking all this time, but Patty hasn't been listening.

She will smear his forehead with menstrual blood, then slice a line in his lower abdomen and rub her face in his blood and guts. And shit. Shit will be smeared everywhere. She will hang him upside down, ankles chained together and thighs smeared with shit. She will leave him there with her formidable dildo in his asshole and slashes in his heels so he cannot walk when she unties him. She will be ruthless and loyal. After she slashes his heels, she will check in with a Baby, Are You Okay? Tell Me You're Okay, and take out his gag so he can say so. Then she will shove the gag back down his throat, kneel before him and masturbate where he can see her, inches from his nose and mouth.

Patty shrugs, smiles lazily over at her date, lost in her dreaming. His tongue in her mouth is slithery and warm, then a lifeless slab of muscle to her weak response. Fumbling and finally dead. Retracted.

Patty clenches and unclenches her thighs, faster, faster, until she is done.

When she is done, she thanks him, saying, "We should do it again sometime."

Then she slams the car door and hurries through the rain to her apartment building, stepping on a slug that's sprawled out to suck in the moisture. Ugh, that squish. She scrapes the slug-guts off on the doorstep and lets herself inside.

There are dishes in the sink. Patty leaves them. She grabs a used glass and fills it with filtered water. Gulps it down. Stands there with her fingers on her lips, thinking he wasn't so bad. She could have been nicer. She could have tried harder. Made something happen. But what had he looked like? She remembers the nervous gurgling in particular. The meek way he cleared his throat. The tapping on the steering wheel, anxious and impatient.

She had made him impatient. That's funny. She had had an effect. He probably would've been too safe in bed, anyway. He would've wanted her to act like a girl.

Everyone is always too safe. What do normal people do? They take off their shoes and makeup and go to bed.

Patty takes off her shoes and makeup and goes to bed. Patty has not closed her window, despite the drizzle, which has now turned to rain. It is raining hard. The rain is hard. Hard rain. Getting harder. The rain is getting harder and harder until it is too hard for anyone to handle.

Patty, close the window! Patty, close the window!

But Patty does not close the window.

Once, a long while ago, Patty was in love with a man she met online. He, rottingdonquix@xxx.com, had responded to an ad, or she had responded to his, and they had had a feverish exchange confessing their own and encouraging one another's perversities. He would write dutifully every morning; she would respond before retiring for the night. In their emails, they would each describe her or his every desire in obsessive detail, carefully crafting fetish after fetish with the intent to elicit the most violent desire and intrigue. For Patty, masturbation had never been so good.

After a time, they began to write erotic stories for each other. Patty wrote rottingdonquix a story modelled on the *Story of O*, in which O grew a cock and turned the tables on her Master, reducing him to the most obsequious and pathetic of slaves. Rottingdonquix responded with a story inspired, she found out later, by Sacher-Masoch, in which his Venus was covered in fur, rather than wearing furs, for she was a vampiric werewolf who feverishly desired to suck the blood from the narrator's cock. Patty wrote him another story in which Bataille's bull's eye is passed back and forth from orifice to orifice until finally, in the midst of passionate intercourse, it bursts in the protagonist's throbbing cunt. He had written back with an overwrought masturbation fantasy revolving around an onyx engagement ring. Upon reading it, she experienced the strong stench of rotten eggs, and could not bring herself to reply.

Weeks passed.

One day, missing the thrill of rottingdonquix's emails, Patty wrote him with the suggestion that they meet in person. He agreed. He was fat and ugly. She left with a sneer on her face. That was the end of love.

Patty is in her bed masturbating. She has tied her date up with fishing line that cuts into his skin, leaves blood blisters pooling subcutaneously. She does the same with his cock, which is always fully erect, engorged even, then kneels in front of him, makes eye contact, and extracts her tongue slowly, torturously, until the tip just touches the head of his cock. He moans behind his gag. Saliva gets stuck in his throat and he tries to clear it, takes two tries, three, is perpetually clearing his throat. Patty's tongue has not moved from its tentative perch on the tip of his cock. Then she lurches forward to wrap it around the head while grabbing the ends of the fishing line with her hand and tugging, gently, gently, until he comes. He comes five more times as she frees his cock from the fishing line.

Patty does not come, because Patty's fantasy is dumb. Mindless SM drivel. Patty can do better. Patty tries again.

Patty is masturbating. Patty grows a cock and it extends, fully engorged and throbbing with sensation. Patty's cock extends and extends, quivering in the air it is exposed in, then slowly curves backward and into her cunt. Patty's cock tentatively probes her cunt before beginning to fuck it, first leisurely, then hard, pummeling it in sync with the hard rain outside. Patty's cock and Patty's cunt come at the same time. Patty comes. Patty drifts off. Patty still has not closed the window. Tap, tap. Tap.

Slug hangs down from the top of the window, suctioning his wet body, his enormous foot, to the exterior pane. There is a loud and sustained *squerk* as Slug navigates the windowpane at his infuriatingly slow pace. Patty stirs from her half-sleep. Two sets of tentacles probe the glass. Tap, tap. Tap.

The incoming air is cold and moist. Patty stirs again, shivers. Her nipples tighten. Slug's tentacles fidget impatiently as they work to gauge the size of the opening. The open window is not wide enough for Slug's impressive girth, but Slug is both lubricated and stretchy. He begins the process of entering her room. Patty blinks.

Slug is six feet of pure muscle struggling to get through her window. Slug is a rippling lump of skin shimmering with beads of rain on top of a more general wetness. Slug is multicoloured, translucent, eyeless, faceless, hairless. Slug's intricate underbelly is lined with undulating muscles that tremble against the pane, excreting stickiness, excreting slime.

Patty, torn between horror and desire, cannot bring herself to look away.

By now Slug has pushed a quarter of his body through the window, attaching himself to the other side of the glass. He pulls himself further forward, inch by thick inch, up the glass until his full length is inside. A pause, a shudder of slick skin, before he continues. He crawls along the wall, staining it with his wet trail as he nears her bed. Hanging down, he fills her nostrils with the smell of fresh soil. His tentacles toy with her hair.

Slug curves toward her, his back end vertical, attached to the wall, his front end suctioning itself to her shoulder, kneading her skin with his underbelly, like an introduction, like saying hello. Patty sucks in her breath.

Hello. He twists toward her head. Soon there is mucus creeping through her hair. His front end gropes her forehead, sticky lubricant oozing into her brows, clumping her eyelashes together, choking her nasal passage with a swamp musk. She opens her mouth to breathe. He enters, gropes around, sucks on her tongue noisily with the front portion of his foot, and pushes forward until her throat closes up and rejects him. He pulls himself out with reluctance, works his way to her torso. Past her chin, along her neck, he slurps noisily, slowly, taking his time. The bedsprings bark. As he moves forward, he shoves her camisole down, the thin straps breaking, and flattens both breasts with his weight, his belly gripping and releasing her nipples rhythmically. She finds herself making soft gurgling sounds deep in her larynx. Slug gurgles in reply.

Then he slugs himself down, less leisurely now, hugging the curves of her abdomen, his tentacles seeking her tunnel. Slowed by an unruly nest of hairs, his lubricant smooths the way, and— at last—he probes her slit, first tentative, then with force. He inches forward, nudging her thighs apart. Patty's hands claw at the sheets. The wind rustles trees outside. The wind enters the room triumphantly, amplifying the scent of swamp that is beginning to suffocate Patty.

Slug surges forward, stretching himself taut, easily eight

feet long, digging, digging as deep as he can, the bed creaking with every insatiable thrust. Lodged inside her vulva, his front half shifts to suit her, curving back and downward. The rest of his body, resting on her torso, kneads her flesh raw. Under his weight, she struggles to further open her thighs. It is difficult—he is massive, his skin so slippery—but she needs to show him: more, please more. She wants all of him. Slug manages to pull a few more inches of his body inside, his trembling underbelly attacking her canal from all angles, speeding its tempo to frantic bursts. Faster. Harder. Her muscles tense. Faster. Harder. Almost. Slug gently chews the insides of her vagina, bringing her to excessive climax. Patty arches, kicks, sucks in so deep she nearly swallows her tongue.

The room is heavy with dampness. Slug slows to a hum. Then he extracts himself slowly, the suction stubborn, painful to break, and rests on top of her, his underbelly engulfing her whole body in its folds.

Slug has crushed Patty.

Slug kisses Patty. Slug kisses Patty until Patty can't breathe. Slug is in her nostrils and mouth. Slug's mucus drips down her throat and fills her lungs. Slug's mucus fills her body. Patty is drenched in Slug, stuck in him, inextricable. Her eyes are slimed shut, her hair slimed into new skin. Her face is slimed into an amorphous blob. Patty tries to move, but Slug's weight prevents her. She chokes a little, learning how to breathe again.

His work done, Slug releases her and crawls up onto the wall behind her. He creeps back over to the window and perches there, his head turning toward her, his tentacles dancing. He emits a gurgle. It seems to mean Come With Me.

Though she cannot see the limbs that are no longer there, Patty understands that her body has changed. She rolls onto her belly, finding that she can feel where she is with two sets of tentacles attached to what used to be her face. She tries to talk but can only gurgle back.

Slug nods; he understands.

Patty follows Slug through the trees behind her apartment building, their slime smoothing them over wet leaves and limp twigs, over thin gravel, the occasional rotting pine cone, until they come to a heavy dampness under a half-fallen tree trunk. Slug turns back and nudges her playfully, his tentacles fondling hers. Then he leads her up the trunk and out onto one of its out-stretched limbs. There they mate, Slug showing her how to wrap around his length as he wraps around hers, so that they are like DNA strands, like corkscrews, hanging down from the limb on one rope of slime. It is easy, like love, this full-body writhing. For a long while they are content to lick each other, lapping up one another's slime and producing more in its place.

This is the wettest Patty has ever been. Her body is in full tremble, every pore of her skin secreting slime, every nerve channelling excitement.

Suddenly she feels a new sensation: her cock is beginning to protrude translucent from her mantle to wrap around Slug's protruding cock, its sensitivity heightened with every tingle of the wind. Like their bodies, their cocks writhe around each other until they are inextricably intertwined. Then their cocks begin to expand, throbbing and massive, together forming an intricate flower that dangles down from their hanging bodies.

Patty and Slug tighten their embrace further and further still, in sync with their pulsating cocks. Tighter, tighter, tighter; their cocks throb, begging for release. Finally they ejaculate, each fertilizing the other in an extended climax that stops time and thought.

Patty is dizzy. Patty is exhausted. But Patty has more work to do.

Because slugs' cocks often get stuck together after mating, the chewing off of one or both cocks is sometimes called for, and because slugs are hermaphrodites, this is totally not a big deal. Because Slug's cock is stuck in Patty's cock, Patty must begin to chew it away, being careful not to chew off her own cock in the process. As Patty gently chews, Slug writhes around her body and gurgles in pleasure, in pain. When she is done, Slug drops down and sprawls on the leaf-matted forest ground for a moment, recovering. Then he creeps away.

Now Patty is alone, dangling precariously from the tree limb. She tries swinging herself over to the trunk but, fatigued, cannot build momentum. Like her lover has done, she allows herself to fall from the rope of slime to the soft ground. Though the fall is not long, the impact stings her still hypersensitive skin.

Here Patty rests. What will Patty do next?

Patty will leave the forest. She will creep back to her home. She will creep back to her bed. But her home can no longer be her home, she knows, for there the air is dry. She must go where the air is moist.

Postulation on the Violent Works of the Marquis de Sade

Elizabeth Bachinsky

> "I am said to have a hard heart, a very bad one
> indeed; but is that fault really mine? or is it not
> rather from Nature we have our vices as well as
> our perfections?"
> —Marquis de Sade, *120 Days of Sodom*

Marquis, right now, a woman in Toronto
is pushing a length of pipe into a man
who is paying her to hate him. It's a strange
appropriation to finance a woman's hatred,
but it's also hard work to put a pipe inside
a man. After he's left her bachelor apartment,
she'll roll her drop sheet back and hose it down
in the tub. She'll peel away her tall plastic
boots and rub her calves. Her shoulders
and her jaw will be sore. She'll take a bath
and, afterwards, she'll make a pot of soup
and eat it while she watches HBO.

What's her transgression, or for that matter,
his? His torture's self-imposed; she'll spend time
in Venice for her holidays, get more time
off than a Safeway clerk will ever have.
It's too easy to call her a victim
and he her oppressor. His pleasure
and her commerce are entwined.
Perhaps it's preferable they marry
so she'll no longer require a paycheque,
but an allowance? This ain't the fifties,
man, though we've still got that atom bomb.
Imagine! That tool exists which, as you say,
"could so assail the sun to snatch it from
the universe and use that star to burn the world."

My terror is terror's ubiquity.
War: it's not murder, it's industry
and a pretty swell career besides.
Think of those sitting on death row
who await appointments with machines,
their last sensation that of a needle's
prick in the vein or a hand to secure
their restraints. It's no sweet sexual game
for the inmate or for the soldier who
might never know their killer's face but who
can put death on their calendar like a
holiday. There is difference between
what is real and what is fantasy.

Marquis, I see you in your cell;
it's cozy, despite the racket in the streets—
all around you, papers and books spread
open like mouths to mouth your fiction.
Outside, the revolution raves while you

have every comfort a man could desire
but freedom, yet there's more—even freedom
is a curse for you. Bourgeois, your own find
you reprehensible, and yet you are far
from a man of the people. Where does one
live when one fits nowhere but in fiction
and insanity? Even today
that's what we call our in-betweens: insane.
We give them lithium and bus passes and hope
they melt into the crowd. I think that, in my time,
you may have loved as you desired. That one
for whom your whip made passage through
the night? She lives, anticipates her agony
one blow at a time—and how she wears her stripes!
Such is the nature of our theatre, to paint
the coward's face with bravery, the bold pallid
with fear.

Further Postulation on the Violent Works of the Marquis de Sade

Elizabeth Bachinsky

> "My passions, concentrated on a single point, resemble the rays of a sun assembled by a magnifying glass: they immediately set fire to whatever object they find in their way."
> — Marquis de Sade, *Juliette*

It's true, I loathe what you would have me love
and, in my loathing, goad your glee the more.
Marquis, my heart, the heart you'd have me have

takes pleasure from such crime there is no salve
to soothe it. Would you have me spell the gore?
It's true, I loathe what you would have me love.

Perhaps you'd like to know that, though we've lived
in such different times, there is no end to terror,
Marquis. My heart, the heart you'd have me have

erased, still quickens. Half the planet starves,
while half the planet fattens; we murder whores.
I can't help loathe what you would have me love:

a vision of the world so dark I'd crave
to be beaten so as not to see the stars.
Marquis, my heart, the heart you'd have me have

must never find its voice. We are not slaves
to vice as kindled wood is slave to fire.
Here is truth. I loathe what you would have me love,
Marquis. My heart can't be the heart you'd have me have.

Conspiracy of Fuckers

Nomy Lamm

"I feel it pressing in on me, this web of fear, trying to own my heart, my sex, my identity ..." My fingers bang on the typewriter keys, pressing out the urgency of the moment. This is the introduction to the ninth issue of my zine, *Conspiracy of Fuckers*. It's been almost a year since the last issue came out, and I've been promising a new one for at least six months. I fear that this kind of writing could get me arrested in this era of surveillance and dictatorship, but I refuse to be silenced. I refuse to let go of what I see as my reality.

Ring! The phone cuts into my reverie.

I should be expecting it, but my heart jumps into my throat and my hands flutter in the air around my chest, my space interrupted. I want to assume that this is a government agent, wanting to derail me from the important manifesto I'm writing. I laugh at myself for taking myself so seriously, and then I get mad at myself for laughing. It *is* serious. I don't know if what I write will ever change anything, but I have to do it to survive. It's all connected.

"Hello?"

"Okay, I have one for you, he's a real nice man. His name is Hugh Billings, he's going to call you because he can't let his wife hear the phone ring." It's the dispatcher for Gentle Tones, the phone-sex company I work for. The most low-tech dinosaur of an operation, they actually have us call the clients instead of connecting us through a computer system. I work for them only because they don't ask for social security numbers, so I don't have to report my wages. I'm not even sure the dispatcher knows my real name; she always calls me Desiree, the alias I use with the callers.

"I'm not really cool with you giving out my home phone number," I tell the dispatcher.

"Well, I could give the call to another girl, but this guy is a regular and he could be a good one for you. Are you sure you want to miss out on it? You might not get another call tonight." She's so manipulative.

"Fine, fine." I hang up and wait for the phone to ring, pounding out the next piece of my manifesto. "We dare not hope to change our misfortune, instead clinging to the hope of feeling something, anything more than what we are told is real ..."

The phone rings.

"Hello?" My voice jumps up half an octave with a little bit of that sleepy gravel I use to make myself sound sexy.

"Heya," I'm greeted by a lilting condescension, hushed, like he's hiding in the basement. "How are you tonight?"

"Mm, I'm good," I purr.

"I bet you're a bad girl," he sputters, and I giggle. "Are you a bad girl?"

"Yeah, I'm a bad little girl."

"Uhhh, I thought so." I can feel him stroking himself with this thought. "I bet you're so young, you don't even have any hair on your pussy. I bet you're touching that little bald pussy right now."

"Mm, you're right, I am," I giggle, secretly rolling my eyes.

"How young?"

"Hmm?"

"How young are you?"

"Eleven?" I won't go younger than that.

"Oooh, you're so bad," he chides. Slap, slap, slap, I hear in the background. "I can just picture you in your room on the bed playing with that little pussy."

"You wanna watch me play with it?" Despite myself, I reach down and start to touch myself My clit is fat and hard, sticking out like a little cock head. I rub it and suck in my breath, moaning for him.

"I love watching you through the door, just slightly open, just a crack. You're lying on your pink canopy bed, you don't know I'm watching you. Oh, you're just so cute, touching yourself. Can you feel it? Do you feel my eyes on you?"

"Mmm, yeah." I feel myself start to space out to avoid the fear that invades my body at the thought of being watched. The shades are down, but I know there are cracks that someone could see through if they wanted to. I look around the room, orienting myself to the familiar things around me. The blue velvet couch. The pink metal typewriter. My cane, leaning against the radiator. The metal brace I strap around my knee to keep it from popping out of joint. I don't look toward the windows.

"Oh, my little girl." I can hear him collapsing in on himself, his voice going far away. "I'm watching you. I can see you. Such a dirty little slut. I love watching my baby girl touch herself."

"Oh, daddy," the word slips out so easy and simple. "I want your big hard cock. I want you in my pussy."

He moans. "I knew it. Daddy's little slut. Showing off for daddy, you're such a bad girl. I should punish you for turning me on like this."

"Oh, daddy, don't hurt me, I didn't mean it."

"I'm gonna teach you a lesson, you little slut."

I wish I could type without him hearing me. I feel words bursting out of me. Resistance: "You can try to force it out of me, but you can't touch my power. Me and my girlfriends, my comrades, my people, we are going to bring this shit-hole patriarchy down.

We are going to align ourselves with the animals and trees and the wind, and after your sorry, self-hating shell of an excuse for a person implodes, we will be here, living in the sunlight and dancing in the dirt."

"Spread those little legs."

"No, daddy, no."

"I said, spread those legs."

"No!"

"Do it!" he growls. "I'm gonna force myself inside that tight little cunt. Oh god, it's so tight. Oh, fuck, so tight and wet and soft. Uh, I love fucking my little girl."

"Oh, daddy, fuck me, fuck me, daddy." I gasp half-heartedly, rubbing my clit, which I imagine to be a cock, sliding inside a tight hole.

"You're gonna make your daddy come, baby. You wanna make me come?"

Ding.

This is the sound of the bell I ring to clear the air after a call, to let go of whatever misgivings I have about the interaction, and go on with my real work.

"We are not going to shrivel under the weight of their pressure. We will harden and brighten, become more focused and intentional, until the force of this brilliance is released and able to become one with its source, which is ultimately love."

I want to cry, but it's stuck inside. Does writing these words actually make me feel less trapped? Does it make me less alone? I have to believe in those people who tell me they get something out of my writing. I have to hope that the fascists won't kill us for seeing what's happening.

I get two more seven-minute calls before my shift ends at two a.m. That makes my income for the night an even twenty dollars. I don't know how to make this profitable for myself when I can barely stand most of my clients. I don't mind the quickies, but the regulars and the guys who want to stay on the phone for hours at a time—the ones who bring in the money—I feel them sucking my spirit. The more they call, the more vulnerable I feel, and I start sabotaging, trying to make them not like me. My last paycheque barely cleared a hundred dollars. I don't know how I will make rent next month.

I climb into bed and cuddle up to my teddy bear, Elfy. I got him when I was six, and in the hospital for the third or fourth time. He has always been my confidant. He knows everything about me, he holds my secrets, he keeps me safe.

CASE #10442289073628MDM84667

NAME: Regina Venquist, a.k.a. "Reggie Vanquish,"
     a.k.a. "Vagina Vanguard"

AGE: 29

RACE: Caucasian (possible Semitic background)

HEIGHT: 5'7"

WEIGHT: 195 lb

DISTINGUISHING CHARACTERISTICS: Walks
     with a cane, wears a leg brace (knee injury due to
     childhood accident, never corrected despite numer-
     ous attempts at reconstruction). Short hair, mascu-
     line appearance.

THREAT LEVEL: Extremist potential. Considers
     herself to be a part of a "revolution" by and for
     homosexuals.

ILLEGAL ACTIVITY: Distribution of written ma-
     terials intended to incite anti-government action.
     Receipt of undocumented funds. Drug use. Sexual
     deviancy.

PLAN OF ACTION: To be determined.

GOAL: Neutralization.

Where am I? I wake up confused. My head feels like a long hallway with footsteps echoing. The hospital. No. I'm here, in my room. I feel watched. I lean over and turn on my light, searching the room with my eyes. Nothing is out of place, but something feels … different. I wrap myself in my robe and hobble out into the living room with Elfy tucked under my arm. "Did you see anything?" I ask him, as I plop down in front of my typewriter. He stares at me with a weird look on his face, but says nothing.

"I feel them watching me," I type. "I can't tell anymore if it's paranoia or reality. There's nobody I can trust to ask. It's true that the government is watching us, tapping our phones, tracking our movements, our purchases, our activities, looking for clues into our weaknesses. It's true that the corporations are not separate from the government, and that any threat to the machine of war, the machine of production, is reason enough to neutralize us."

Neutralize. That's exactly what they want to do. Make us neutral so that we can't advocate for ourselves, can't fight, can't impact or change anything. My body tingles with connections being made. I feel powerful, but scared.

I hold Elfy tight to my chest, but it doesn't help. Something is weird about him. I hold him so he's facing me and stare into his eyes. "What is wrong with you?" He stares back hard and cold. He's never looked at me like that before.

I stash him in the closet and close the door, but immediately feel guilty. Whatever is going on with Elfy right now, it's not his fault. He's probably as confused as I am. I wish there was someone I could talk to about this. Everyone would think I'm crazy. I open the closet door and take him back out, stare in his eyes again. I look over at my typewriter, where I usually bare my soul in order to make myself feel better, but I can't say this, even in a zine. My stuffed bear has been possessed by the government? I need some sleep.

I tie a bandana around Elfy's eyes, apologize to him, and climb back into bed, pulling him close to my chest. It's 7:30 a.m., and the sun is glaring off the snow outside, exploding through the cracks around the slatted blinds. I fall into a deep, dreamless sleep.

I've been at the copy shop for two hours now, finishing up the new issue of my zine so I can send it out. It's getting harder these days to steal photocopies, but luckily I know a code for the machine because I used to have a friend who worked here. The zine is fat, hard to fold, impossible to staple. I am proud and nervous about putting this out into the world. I have tried to stay true, even though the circumstances of the world have gotten so much harder since this regime stole the election. I put the zine up to my nose and sniff, taking in that fresh copy smell. So many memories. We used to come in big groups, idealistic punks believing nothing could stop us. Now I come alone. Nobody my age wants to do things like this anymore. The younger people are too busy on their computers; this wouldn't even occur to them.

The sun is long gone by the time I leave the copy shop, undetected, my bag heavy with secrets. I have to be home by six p.m. to start work. I've been getting a lot of calls lately, my mind is a fog of simulated sex. I clank down the street, grateful that most of these people see me as a teenage boy. I don't want the attention of men. I rub the stubble on my chin with satisfaction.

The phone is ringing as I walk in the door. It's not even six yet.

"Hello?" I say in my normal voice, expecting the dispatcher.

"Heya." It's Hugh, my new regular. "I was hoping you would be home."

"Oh, hey," I say, as if I'm glad to hear from him, softening into my girly voice. "I just got home from school."

"I didn't know you were in school," he says with interest. "What are you studying?"

"History," I choose something close enough to what I actually care about, hoping he won't ask too many questions.

"A very important subject," he says. "The founding of this great nation, all that good stuff."

"Totally," I say, clenching my jaw in order to avoid mentioning genocide and slavery. "Is your cock hard, daddy?"

"Oh, you know it is baby." His breath comes out in a shivering gasp. "I've been saving it for you. Ever since I got home from work I've been hard, trying to hide it from my wife."

"You don't want to have sex with her?" I undo the strap on my brace and take it off, leaning it against the arm of the couch, rubbing my knee, which is swollen and sore from all the walking I had to do today.

He laughs. "No, she's an old hag. I never get hard for her."

"I see." I'm supposed to be flattered.

"You like that?"

"Sure," I say, feeling gross for conspiring against another woman. I buy time by breathing and going "mmm" into the receiver, thinking about what to say next. "I want you to save it all for me."

"Oh, you know I will, baby girl. I got a big load for you tonight."

I giggle.

"You know I've been spying on you, every night, I've been watching you in your bedroom when you think you're all alone."

"You have?" My body goes cold. I hate this fantasy.

"I've been peeking in your door when it's not all the way closed, and one night when it was closed tight I went around the house and stood in the bushes outside your window. I could see you from a perfect angle, your little hand between your legs while you played with yourself."

My moans are automatic. I quietly unzip my bag and pull out the stack of zines. *Conspiracy of Fuckers,* they read across the top, juxtaposed with a photocopy of barbed wire. I smirk, remembering the way it scratched up the surface of the photocopier.

"I'm glad nobody caught me jerking off in front of your window, that sure would have been embarrassing." He laughs.

"Yeah, totally." I giggle. I hope he's not catching on that I'm not really paying attention. I reach into my bag for a pen and pull a stack of yellow envelopes from under the coffee table.

"I can't believe you've been watching me touch myself. I'm so embarrassed," I say, playing along with his creepy game. I take a pain pill and wait for it to hit me, to take off the rough hard edges.

Forty-five minutes later he comes, and I get off the phone, dinging my bell to clear the air. I call the dispatcher to make sure she knows how long we went.

"You just did a call with Hugh Billings? I didn't authorize that."

"Are you kidding me?" The life drains out of me and I feel nauseous.

"I told him you weren't signed on yet."

"I just did an hour long call with him."

"Look, you should never do a call unless I authorize it first," she scolds.

Rage rises up in my body. I want to point out that it was her awesome idea to give him my phone number, instead of the other way around, like we do with most clients. I stay calm, stammering through my explanation. I need her to pay me for this call.

"I'll try to work it out," she says, and we hang up the phone. I stuff envelopes and write addresses on them, trying not to want to die.

A few minutes later, the phone rings again.

"Hello?" I expect to hear the dispatcher's voice.

"Boy, you just got me in a shit load of trouble. Thanks a lot." It's him. There's a pushy, controlling edge to his voice.

"You're not supposed to call me unless you get authorization from dispatch first."

"That bitch just called my house and my wife answered," he says, as if I'm supposed to feel bad about it.

"Did you pay for this call? Because the dispatcher should have called me first."

"No, I'm not calling to get you off again, you little slut, I'm calling to scold you for getting me into a big pile of steaming shit." There is no way I am taking this role play into an actual relationship with him.

"That's not my problem," I say, and hang up quickly. I'm shaking. I go in the bedroom and grab Elfy. He seems to have gone back to normal in the past week; I don't know what was wrong with me the night he seemed possessed. Holding him close, I pick up the phone to call the dispatcher.

"Hugh Billings just called me again," I tell her.

"You didn't do the call, did you?"

"Of course not."

"Okay, well, he's cut off now."

"I'm afraid to answer the phone. What if he calls again?"

"Don't you have caller ID?"

"No."

"What age are you living in?"

"The government uses caller ID to monitor our calls."

"You're crazy, that doesn't even make sense."

I hang up feeling defeated and terrified. I take another pain pill, smoke a bowl, and snuggle up on my couch in my robe with a baseball bat next to me to make me feel more secure. Every time the phone rings I expect to hear his voice, but it's just the dispatcher. I get four more calls before the end of my shift and go to bed in a haze of blended realities.

CASE #10442289073628MDM84667

UPDATE: Engaged in theft of photocopies to re-
produced booklets of incendiary materials, with
intent to disseminate. *(Conspiracy of F**kers,* see
attached copy.) Earned several hundred dollars
in unclaimed income. Purchased marijuana and
counterfeit prescription narcotics. Enacted incestu-
ous pedophile role-play fantasies in the employ of
Gentle Tones.

ASSESSMENT: A solid case has been built on the
basis of drug trafficking, theft, sexual deviancy, and
potential anti-government/anti-commerce terrorist
activity.

RISK: Low. Suspect is weak and will be easy to neutralize. Begin process of neutralization ASAP.

Ring!

"No!" I bolt out of my sleep, sitting straight up in bed. My
heart is racing, and all I can hear is the blood pumping in my
head. I look at the clock next to my bed. It's three a.m. After
six rings, the voicemail picks up. I sit alert in the dark, attuned
to every noise in the apartment: a creak from the living room, a
scurrying sound in the corner.

A minute later, it begins to ring again. Six rings, then silence.
And then again.

I get out of bed and go out into the living room where the
phone is. The room is pitch black, but I am afraid to turn on the
light. I feel a presence around me and don't want to be seen.

I wrack my brain trying to think of someone I can call for
help. I want to call my recent ex, but that doesn't seem like a
good idea. Nobody else comes to mind. Just acquaintances, a
couple girls I've slept with, and people I haven't seen in months.

After the phone has been silent for a minute, I pick it up, put it
to my ear, and begin dialling. But there is no dial tone.

"Hello?" I say suspiciously.

"You think you can hide from me?" His voice is right there, waiting for me, slithering into my ear like a parasite. I slam the phone down quickly. I lift it again and tap the lever, trying to get a dial tone.

"I'm still here, you little slut, you think you can fuck with me like this and I'm just gonna take it? Fuck you, whore."

I hold down the receiver and count to thirty before picking it up. As I get to twenty-nine, the phone starts ringing again. I'm approaching a max-out point where it all starts to be funny. Is this real?

"Leave me the fuck alone, I'm calling the police!" This is an ironic threat, coming from me, but hopefully he'll take it seriously.

"I'm watching you, slut. I know where you live."

"Fuck OFF!" I scream into the phone, slamming it down hard. I pick it up again and slam it back down, over and over again—seven, eight times—until, finally, I get a dial tone. I dial the only number that knows how to come out of me: My ex, Josiah Bird.

"Hello?" his voice is all sleepy, and I picture him in his comfy bed.

"Oh thank god."

"What do you want," he asks in a flat tone. But I know he will come over if I really need him. And I really do.

"Are you doing okay, like, in general? Have you eaten? Are you sleeping? How much pot have you been smoking?" It's just like Josiah to try to approach the problem like it's a matter of health.

"Look, Josiah. I don't know." I say the words slowly and deliberately. Can't he see that I'm completely consumed with terror right now? "This guy won't leave me alone; I feel like he knows exactly what I'm doing, like he really is right outside my window looking in."

Josiah walks to the door, opens it, and looks outside. I cringe.

"There's nobody there." He comes back over to me, takes my hand and pulls me off the couch. "Let's go see what you've got in the kitchen. You hungry?"

"I don't know," I follow him in and watch him boil a pot of water and pour oatmeal into it. He slices up an apple and adds a few shakes of cinnamon. This was one of the best things about dating Josiah. He's magic with food. This oatmeal is perfect, not a glop of gruel, but delicately textured, perfectly softened individual grains, warm and smooth and sweet. I savour each spoonful as I swallow it down, and feel my body relax into the moment. Things start to feel familiar again.

The first thing Josiah did when he got here was turn off the ringer on my phone. The second thing he did was call the police, which I begged him not to do. "They won't come here, Reggie, I promise, I've done this before. They just take a report over the phone, and if he keeps calling they can track it."

The sun starts to come up. "I really need to get some sleep," he says.

"Okay." I guess it feels safe now.

"I can sleep here on the couch."

"Oh." I look down at the floor. "You can sleep in my bed if you want."

We stare into each other's eyes. There is warmth there, and defensiveness.

"All right," he says, heaving himself off the couch. "But I gotta get some sleep, okay? No funny business!"

"What? Me?" I laugh, and it feels good, loosening the constricted feeling in my ribcage. "I'll try to restrain myself."

We climb under the covers and each roll to our separate sides of the bed. For the first time in a week I fall into a deep sleep, with no bad dreams. No dreams at all.

I wake up on fire. Hot, heavy breathing in my ear, Josiah's body pressed up against me, rubbing relentlessly. My body is involved before my brain knows what is going on, returning his grinding motions, reaching back and around his head to hold him close, breathing hard into his hair. I turn toward him slowly, feeling the intensity building inside me without even being touched. My heart feels huge and open, desperately reaching out toward his for connection.

His leg slips between mine, and I feel his little cock grinding against my thigh through his boxers, all hard and swollen. My whole body shudders at the feel of it, and I wonder if he can feel my clit, too. It's not as big as his, but I have been using a clit pump to try to make it bigger and more sensitive. He bites my neck and growls as I run my hands down his back and up under his shirt. He rolls on top of me and for the first time we look at each other, our hips still moving. I pull his shirt up and touch his now-unfamiliar chest with my hand. His new scars are fresh, pink, and raised. He had surgery right after we broke up. I thought I would never get to feel this body.

To my surprise, my eyes are welling up. He smiles. I feel exposed, sentimental, and start thrusting my hips harder at him to show him it's a serious ride. I reach my hands up around his back and scrape my short-but-sharp nails over his skin. He winces.

"You like that?" He nods.

I slap his face. He smiles.

I flip him over on his back, lay next to him, and slide my hand into his boxers, rubbing my hand in his wetness to lube up my fingers, sliding back over his cock, giving him a nice wet hand job. He groans and his ass tightens, lifting his hips up off the bed. "Fuck me?" He stares into my eyes with that pained look he gets when he's desperate to come.

Smiling, I slide two fingers up inside him, rubbing his g-spot while circling his cock-head with my thumb. He groans and moves his body in time with my hand. He grabs the hair on the back of my head and pulls, whimpering and pleading for me to make him come. "Please, oh fuck, you're gonna make it happen, it's coming."

I fuck him with the muscle of my whole arm and synch up the flow so that his body can bounce along with me, both of us released into the laws of physics. "I wanna see you come, I wanna watch your face," I say in a low voice that echoes through my body, the vibration sending nice little shock waves to the head of my clit. He puts his hand between my legs. It's turned the wrong way, and he can't pay attention to what he's doing anyway, but he moves it around, and I hump my body against him so he rubs me just right as I push another finger up inside him.

My orgasm builds as I watch him fall into his. His groans get louder and longer and his face contorts into a pained, then overwhelmed expression before it dissolves into surrender and his whole body bucks up, heaving and shaking, his cunt spasming around my three fingers. My whole body feels hot and fuzzy, like the borders of it have faded, and colours flood my mind, red and purple, and then a bright orange light exploding through me, emanating from my clit, up into my pelvis, my gut, my heart. Burning its way through the hard, stuck places, chasing out the fear.

I hold him tight, sweating against his skin, shudders passing through me, through us. I am overwhelmed. I'm glad I can't cry, because I don't want him to see me like that, I don't want him to feel too needed, or think I'm putting too much on this. I know we aren't in love, that it didn't work. But I've never had this feeling with anyone else. It's been hard to give up.

"Did you notice anything different?"

We're sitting on the couch again in the living room. We just ate delicious sandwiches with steamed beets, sauerkraut, and goat cheese. I never would have thought to put those foods together, but he found them and made something amazing out of it. Our tongues are bright pink from the beets, and we're huddled by the radiator trying to keep warm.

"What do you mean?" He looks at me, his eyes guarded, trying to discern my agenda before it's dumped on him.

"I mean, about my body." I wonder what he will think.

He chuckles. "Uh, I wasn't really looking. You feel a little different. That usually happens after a breakup."

I pull the clit pump from under the couch where I keep it. It looks intense and medical, with a hand pump and a dial to indicate how much suction is being created. But when I pull it out, something else comes tumbling onto the floor: a prescription bottle half-full of OxyContin, with someone else's name on it. He grabs it before I can push it back into hiding.

His face falls. His eyebrows scrunch up, and he shakes his head. "Are you shitting me?"

"I've been in a lot of pain."

"Why don't you go to a doctor?"

"You know how I feel about doctors."

"Yeah, and you know how I feel about fucking around with this kind of shit. This is an opiate." Josiah is protective of the work he's done to get sober, which I respect. I've never done opiates before, but my dealer told me this is the best painkiller there is, and my knee has been killing me lately. It's been helping.

"I really don't like the way you're talking to me." We stare hard at each other, our eyes meeting in combat.

"It looks like it's time for me to leave." He sighs and gets up off the couch, grabbing his coat and scarf.

"Fine." We never know how to get through moments like this. We're both too proud, too righteous about our beliefs. That was originally what drew us to each other, but ultimately it was the reason we weren't compatible.

"Do you need anything else before I—"

"Nope," I interrupt. He grabs his bag and leaves in a huff, making a big deal out of not slamming the door on his way out, which I find even more annoying than if he'd slammed it.

I busily shuffle the piles of yellow envelopes around on my coffee table, separating them into addressed and non-addressed, priority and non-priority. I don't know when I'll ever be able to afford to send all these zines out anyway. Fuck the government. Fuck the world. Fuck Josiah.

My hands stop at an empty envelope, addressed to Alex Asshole in Pittsburgh, PA. I remember stuffing this envelope because I was pressing down too hard on the anarchy symbol in "Asshole," and broke through the thick yellow paper, making a mark on the zine. The hole is still there. The zine is not.

The phone rings, and my body fills with dread. Did I turn the ringer back on? I pick up the receiver and hold it to my ear, saying nothing.

"It's me," says Josiah. "I turned the ringer back on while you were still sleeping. Sorry if I scared you."

"Oh." I start to breathe again.

"I didn't want to leave before talking about your plan for tonight. Are you still planning on working?"

"I don't know." I hadn't even thought about it yet. The past twenty-four hours is a blur. "You know, it's okay if you want one of my zines, but I wish you had asked instead of just taking one."

"What zine?"

My stomach drops. "*Conspiracy of Fuckers*. The new issue. I made the exact number I needed, but I didn't think I would see you."

"I didn't even know you made a new issue."

"But ..." My head is going to explode. "There's one missing."

"You probably did something with it."

"No, I remember."

"Reggie, we both know your memory isn't as good as you think it is."

I can't believe he would question my sanity at a time like this. This means my fears are true. I'm being watched, I'm being tracked. Someone came in here while I was sleeping and stole a copy of my zine. I tell him this, trying not to yell.

I hear him take a deep breath to steady himself. "If you really think that's what happened, then you should come over to my place, at least for the night."

"Can I work from your house?"

Josiah groans. Doing phone sex with him in the same apartment was always an issue—he'd hear me and get turned on, but when I'd get off the phone I just wanted to distance myself from it. He always complained about blue balls.

"I'll go in the pantry. I'll be really quiet."

"Whatever. Just get over here. But no drugs."

I smoke a bowl and pop an OxyContin before I leave the house, just to numb the pain so I can make it to the train and up and down all the stairs.

I tell the dispatcher that Hugh Billings was harassing me all night. She seems perplexed. "He's never done that before, and I've been working with him for years."

"It was terrifying."

"Well, he can't come to your house or anything. He lives three states over, and he doesn't know where you live. You shouldn't be scared." She's nice to me, gives me lots of calls, doesn't give me shit for working from another phone number, which she used to always get annoyed about. I spend half the night huddled at the back of Josiah's pantry, cupping my hand around my mouth and the receiver.

"Are you hiding from someone?" one of my clients asks. "You sound muffled."

"My husband's home," I tell him. "I don't want him to hear us."

"Oh no," his voice gets quiet too, and I smile at how silly and sweet this job is sometimes, like playing house as a little kid. "I hope he doesn't hear me fucking you," he says, whimpering. "I hope I can come before he catches us."

"I hope so too. You better fuck me harder."

"Oh, yeah, I'm fucking you so hard, I'm slamming my big hard cock up into your tight wet hole."

"Sshh, he'll hear us," I whisper.

"Ooooh, no," he groans.

"Oh shit, I think I hear him! He's coming! He's gonna catch us!"

He shoots his load, gurgling in my ear. "Oh, fuck, oh fuck," he gasps.

"That was a close one," I smile.

"Thanks. Have a good night." He hangs up.

"Anything good?" Josiah asks as I emerge from the pantry for the fifth time. He's putting sheets on an air mattress in the living room for me. I guess he doesn't want a repeat of last night.

"That one was kind of fun. We pretended my husband was about to catch us."

"Ha!" Josiah shakes his head, probably thinking about my fondness for the we're-gonna-get-caught fantasy. "I bet you liked that one."

I blush. "Yeah." I smile and look at the blanket he's spreading out for me. I remember that blanket. "It definitely gave me a boner." I look up at him to see his reaction. He's shaking his head, trying not to smile.

"Remember how it was when I first started hormones?" he asks, laughing. "I'd be running into the bedroom every time you got a call."

"Yeah." I feel nervous talking about sex too much. I really liked last night. It would be easy for me to fuck him again.

"Okay, well ..." he looks at the floor. "I guess I'm going to bed. Your bed's all made up whenever you're ready."

"I'm ready, I just need to brush my teeth."

I'm glad to see my old toothbrush is still here. I stand over the toilet brushing my teeth while he takes out his contacts and washes his face. My thigh brushes his ass as I lean over to spit into the sink, and I feel him press back into me in response. I can't help it, my hand grabs onto the meat right above the waistband of his pajamas, and slides down over his ass before pulling away. He turns to face me, our eyes lock.

"Don't touch me," he says, taking a step toward me so my back is pushed up against the cupboard door. His face is just a couple inches from mine, our bellies touching. He smirks.

"Okay," I say, keeping my hands at my sides. He leans in like he's going to kiss me, and I lean forward to meet him.

"I said *don't*." He grabs my throat, slamming my head back against the cupboard.

"Sorry," I gasp. He smacks my face fast five or six times, and I snap at him, trying to catch his fingers with my teeth. He grabs my hair with his other hand, pulling my head to the side, subduing me.

"What exactly are you asking for right now?"

"I can't help it." I whine.

"Because you know what you'll get if you keep pushing."

I actually don't know. It could be a struggle down to the ground ending in a vicious, guttural fuck. Or it could be an endless, painful tease. Or it could be a hard wall of nothing. I have to press my luck just enough to stay engaged in the dynamic, but not enough to seriously piss him off. "I thought you said no funny business."

"You started it." He's still got my head twisted to the side, and he reaches between my legs with his other hand, making a pinching motion that catches my clit between his thumb and forefinger, stroking it through my boxer briefs. I groan in response, and without meaning to, my hands move up to his shoulders. He pinches my clit hard and pulls my head further down to the side.

"Okay, okay, I'm sorry, I'm sorry." My eyes bug out and my thighs clamp together trying to protect my clit. This is actually really hurting my neck, and my leg can't hold me like this for too much longer. Still grasping my clit, he pulls me by the hair, directing me to rest my ass on the edge of the sink. "I gotta see this," he says, pulling down my underwear. He pushes back on my cunt lips so that my little cock pokes its head out, all swollen and bright pink. His tongue reaches out to taste it, and I shiver and moan, cursing and trying not to hyperventilate.

He wraps his lips around it and starts to bob his head. I've been working hard to get my clit bigger, pumping it up at least a few times a week, and I can feel so much more than I used to. His mouth is wet and warm; the suction pulling me in so I can feel it in the shaft and the head. It's almost too much, but I keep breathing and it keeps feeling better and better. I want so bad to put my hand on his head and push him down on me, but I know this would get me in trouble, and I don't want to fuck this up.

"Suck it," I say under my breath. He stops, looks up at me, and puts his finger to his lips.

"This is my game. I do what I want." He puts his mouth close to my cock again and I am straining my butt muscles, trying to push it into his mouth, feeling his hot breath. He keeps his mouth right there, just breathing, and I swear the breath is making my cock throb and swell, trying to get bigger so it will reach his wet lips. I am groaning and swearing and losing all control.

"You better be quiet or you're gonna wake up my roommate," he teases, knowing his roommate doesn't care and will probably happily wank off if he wakes up to the sound of sex. But this added bit of intrigue is almost too much for me. I know I'm going to come the second his lips touch me again, and I don't know if I will be able to keep myself from clawing into his shoulders, pushing him down on my cock, and riding his face for all he's worth. I make the decision to do everything I can to control myself, to let him have all the power. He deserves it.

As if he can read my mind, he chooses that moment to finish me off. Warm, wet lips gently subsume the head of my cock and tenderly suck, and I am gone. Shuddering, moaning, tensing and thrusting, doing everything I can to keep my hands to myself. I accidentally knock the soap and shaving kit off the back of the sink, shatter a glass onto the floor, still gripping the edge of the sink while my body spasms. "Fuck," I grunt as the orgasm runs its course and leaves me weak and panting.

Josiah wipes his face on me, smearing my wetness against my belly, then gets up and walks out. I pant and heave and wonder what I should do, struggling to regain my mind. He returns a minute later with a broom and dustpan, and sweeps up the broken glass without saying anything to me. I watch, still recovering.

Just as I'm about to open my mouth to try to say something, he says, "Have a good night," winks, and leaves again. I hear the pantry door, footsteps down the hall, and then the click of the door to his bedroom.

I float on the air mattress, missing Elfy, trying to wrap my head around all that's happening. My knee is throbbing, and I wish I could take another pill. I am having sex with my ex again. One of my phone sex clients is stalking me. Someone stole a copy of my zine from my apartment, and Josiah says it's not him. I want to be able to put all of this together into a big picture, but my mind races from one thing to the other, trying to retrace my steps, trying to find the missing piece that makes me feel a little less confused and terrified.

How will I survive?

In the morning, Josiah and I have another argument over a breakfast of blueberry waffles. We've only been hanging out again for two days, and already I'm getting sick of his shit. He wants an organized, rational plan, he wants to know what's "really" going on, and all I can tell him is a bunch of weird shit keeps happening, and I'm worried they're about to get me. I shouldn't have told him about the night when Elfy was looking at me weird, but he was pushing me for examples and it just came out. I thought at least on a psychic level he would understand that there's something fucked up going on, but he just rolled his eyes.

"Were you high?" he asks. I was, but I don't see what that has to do with it.

"I should have known you would blame it on me. You're such a fucking traditionalist, you want to believe the easy explanations. Why can't you see that things really are as bad as we were afraid they would get? It's all connected, they're trying to hide it from us, they want to separate us so they can bring us down." My voice gets higher, more hysterical.

"Okay, if the government is stalking you, and, as you seem to believe, posing as a phone-sex client, and then sneaking into your apartment to steal a zine in the middle of the night, and turning your stuffed animal against you, then what do you want from me? What can I do for you, besides get sucked into your paranoid story?"

I scream through gritted teeth and slam my fist down on the table. How am I supposed to know? The first thing I'd like is to be believed.

"I'm going to have to ask you to leave," he says, his face turned to stone.

I scoot my chair back from the table and clunk into the living room, grabbing my cane, my bag, and my jacket, leaving the air mattress and blankets in a big messy heap on the floor. I curse the stairs on the way down to the street, my knee aching and pounding.

By the time I get home I am crying from the pain in my knee. I feel broken. I'm fucking pissed that we have this fascist government that uses the money that should go to health care on war and spying on its own citizens. I'm fucking pissed that the only work available to a person with a disability is mind numbing and soul sucking. I'm fucking pissed that queer people don't know how to support each other.

I take a pain pill and fall into bed.

My dreams are missing. They are not mine anymore.

CASE #10442289073628MDM84667

UPDATE: Consistent drug use. Taking steps to send anti-government propaganda to terrorist cells across state lines. Deviant sexual relations with former drug addict posing as opposite gender.

ASSESSMENT: Patterns of behaviour pose a potential threat not only to government and commerce, but to society at large.

CONCLUSION: Neutralization in process, effective immediately.

I wake up at six p.m., and it's already dark out. It's time for me to sign on to work. My mind feels heavy and murky, my whole body is aching, and I feel nauseous. I lurch toward the kitchen and pour myself a bowl of cereal. The crunching sound hurts my head. I catch a glimpse of myself in the mirror as I pass the bathroom, and have to go back and look. In the dim light, I look old, my face hollowed out with shadows, eyes deep in my skull. I see what is happening, but it feels so far away now. I move into the living room to sign on to work, gritting my teeth against the pain in my knee and my head.

"Hi, it's Desiree, signing on for work," I slur into the phone.

"Are you okay?" The dispatcher actually sounds concerned.

"Yeah, just tired."

"All right, I'll let you know if I get anything for you."

I plop down on the couch with Elfy clutched to my chest. He doesn't feel alive, just a lump of fluff. I feel silly holding him; I'm almost thirty. I pick up one of the envelopes on the coffee table and pull my zine out. It looks corny to me, like it's trying so hard to be something. I stare at the photocopied barbed wire, an obvious metaphor, sloppily executed. That's not how I wanted it to look. I open it, flip through, and land on a page with a drawing of a girl with big dark sockets and little shrunken eyes.

"You won't even notice it when they come for you," it reads. "It will happen at the kitchen table, or in the bathtub, or at the grocery store, or watching TV. You will decide that you might as well be satisfied. At least you haven't been bombed, or put in prison. Yet. (Or maybe you have.) Or maybe you got hurt some other way, trapped or sabotaged. Maybe there's someone else who should pay for it. Maybe you should just be grateful for the government's protection. Just join them and be glad you get to."

I won't let that happen to me. I won't be neutralized as long as I am paying attention to what's happening. I'll just keep watching and describing, believing—because I have to—that they can't take me from inside myself.

I do three routine phone-sex calls before Hugh calls me. When he does, I answer it in my phone sex voice, without meaning to. "You knew it was me, didn't you?" His voice sounds so close. I slam the phone down, my heart racing. I pick it up and try to get a dial tone, but the line is silent.

"I called the police on you," I say to the air on the other end. It feels like a flimsy threat.

The line is quiet. I tap the lever one-two-three times. I hold it down for seven seconds. I listen again for a dial tone.

"Hello?" I ask.

Quiet.

"I'm not alone, my boyfriend is here. He's really strong." I am quiet again, wondering if he can feel through my lie. I decide to elaborate. "I'm not afraid." I don't want him to think I feel weak. "I'm not afraid of you." I say again, trying to sound assertive, hearing my voice rising with panic. "Stop calling me. I called the police and I'm calling them again as soon as I hang up."

I hear a muffled sound. He's laughing at me.

Before I can feel the crux of my fear, everything just lets go. Like it's all fire and molten lava, a boiling soup with no barrier between myself and anything else. I hear a loud sound; it's hurting my ears, but it's my own scream. I am still screaming when Josiah answers the phone.

"What!" He shouts. "What's going on?"

I stop, confused. "I didn't call you."

"Obviously, you did. What is going on?"

"Josiah, they just connected me to you, I swear I didn't call you, my hand didn't even touch the phone." In my mind I see an image of my hand moving over the keypad, and change my mind. "Maybe I did. I don't remember. It was him, he was on the other line, and he wouldn't go away, and he was laughing."

"Did you call the police? They should have him on file, and after three reported calls they'll issue him a warning."

"That's not going to help!" I try to keep myself from freaking out on him. I need him. "You have to help me. I need you."

"Actually, this isn't a good time."

We are both silent.

"They're all over me," I whisper.

Josiah sighs. "Reggie, they're not. I promise you. I know you don't want to hear this, but you're going to be okay. You're scared right now, but nobody's going to get you."

As he speaks, a terrible truth starts to dawn on me. "You're one of them, aren't you?"

Josiah groans and laughs. "Yeah, fine, Reggie. If that's what you want to believe."

"Josiah, please. Don't you remember?" I am crumbling. "It's me."

"Like I said, I really don't have time for this." The line clicks, and I tear the cord out of the wall before waiting to see if there's a dial tone.

I grab my aluminum baseball bat and hurtle toward the front door. I push the heavy recliner from the living room, lunging in front of the door. I pull a blanket from the closet and drape it over the windows, covering the cracks of the blinds. I turn off all the lights in the front room and clomp into my bedroom, curling up with the bat next to me, listening to all the night sounds.

They can't get you if you keep watching. Stay alert. Stay present. I don't sleep. Not that I remember.

Someone is calling my name. *Regina*. From the depths of my most buried self a dull innocence, a search for recognition rises. "I'm here." *Regina*. "Come find me." *Regina*. "Come in." I'm swimming through something thick, a warm syrupy liquid that encapsulates me. Where am I? Am I born? Whose body am I in? And then there is a wall. I want to pass through it because there is something beautiful on the other side. I want to touch it, hold it, see what it is. What is this membrane, this separation? Let me have the pretty glimmering self-thing. I want it.

My eyes open in terror to find my body moving without my consent. The sensation in my skin is both hot and cold at the same time, and it's a friction, a moving, both within and without.

"Oh, you're such a good girl, such a sweet little girl." Hot man-breath on my cheek; his chest pressed down on me, stealing my breath. I feel him moving inside me and my body is reaching up to him, meeting his thrusts, sucking him into me, hungry for more, trying to touch the promise dangled in front of my heart. Safety. Protection. Comfort. Be mine.

"Oh, you feel so good," he groans into me. I feel warm and open and cold and distant, all at once. "So nice and wet, such a sweet wet little pussy."

Over his shoulder in the dark corner of the room I notice a tiny red light. A camera's black form makes itself visible against the rest of the dark. It enters my reality smoothly, like the punch-line to a joke I heard years ago.

My body turns animal against me, trying to break through the layer of control. I wrap my legs up around him and pull him in harder and deeper, moaning as my back lifts up off the bed. He breathes hard on my nipple as he licks and sucks, grunting, "Oh my little girl, such a good little girl, oh you feel so good." I reach my arms around him, his broad, muscled back, cringing at the tufts of coarse hair and waxy raised bumps under my fingers. I dive further in, pushing off from the bed and rolling over on top of him. I feel my knee crushing in on itself, but the pain is far away and meaningless. I bounce and grind on top of him, squeezing the muscles in my cunt, watching his face. Not an attractive face: bulbous, undefined features, visible nose hairs, unruly eyebrows, a high forehead with an unconvincing comb-over, splotchy grey five-o'clock shadow. But something about him is appealing, the way his material form slips away into powerless pleasure. I slide up and down on his penis. It twitches inside me as his eyebrows knit up and his mouth opens to reveal dull yellow teeth. I observe as though from a great distance, barely feeling any sensation in my body, only my determination.

CASE #10442289073628MDM84667

UPDATE: Neutralization successful.

I wake up with a vague sense that something has happened, but I can't remember what. Thinking about it doesn't feel good, it makes my stomach seize up and my head throb. I feel disgusting, open and bloated with need, seeping bile. Getting out of bed, my knee collapses on me and I have to push it back into joint. *Fuck.* That old deep body shame weighs heavy on me as I hobble to the living room for my brace.

When I step through the doorway a light flashes in my head that paralyzes me. Everything looks normal. The furniture is all in place. Blinds are drawn up, sunlight streaming in onto smooth surfaces.

I sit down on the couch next to the radiator and start buckling myself into my brace. I stare at the shiny pink typewriter in front of me. I see a flash of my hands on the keyboard, get a sense of déjà vu. I lean toward the feeling but can't locate it.

I look out at the people and cars moving through the snow-covered street. They all seem okay. I need to stop feeling sorry for myself. I should work harder and be nicer to people. Stop blaming everyone else for my problems.

Every Dark Desire

Fiona Zedde

Belle woke up thinking about murder. Well, it really wouldn't be murder since the vampire was already dead, wasn't she? She stared down at Silvija in their shared bed. The beast was beautiful, there was no denying that, in the quiet darkness of the bedroom. Silvija lay with her head back against the sheets, showing off the fine curve of her neck, strong jaw line, and the feathery brush of her eyelashes against her cheeks. Julia lay against her breasts, smiling in demon sleep, a hand splayed possessively over Silvija's muscled belly.

Belle pulled away from them, although her skin nearly groaned at the loss of contact. The sun was still high outside the windows, and the day warm. She knelt in the bed, watching in silence, wanting to rip the skin from the beast's face and feed it to Julia before burning them both to hell. How possible was it? As quickly as the thought brushed through her mind, she was leaning over Silvija and slashing down with a clawed hand. The beast's eyes flew open and she jerked out of Belle's path. Her fingers sliced through the sheets, and before she could adjust her balance, the beast was up from under Julia and behind Belle, her hands grabbing roughly at Belle's upper arms and immobilizing her. The other beasts in the bed didn't stir, she was so quiet.

"What am I going to do with you, puppy?" she hissed, her lips a mere breath from Belle's.

Obviously, the question was purely rhetorical. Silvija quietly lifted her up from the bed without even a grimace of effort and dragged Belle through the house, past the open doors of the other bedrooms, through the dark sitting room, and down even darker stairs to a room that smelled like blood and iron. She locked the door behind them.

"I've tried to be patient with you." While Silvija was preoccupied with the lock, Belle twisted away and tried to run. The beast back-handed her and she slipped down the half dozen steps, landing on her back with a grunt. Then the beast was over her, lifting her up and twisting her hands behind her back before propelling her backward toward the strong iron smells.

"I've tried to be *nice* to you." With quick, efficient movements, she shackled Belle with the dangling manacles and leg irons on the floor.

"What the fuck are you doing?" Belle looked around in alarm.

She was in a damn dungeon straight out of a horror movie with thick brick walls, a torture rack on the far side of the room and, near the far wall, two sets of manacles hanging from the ceiling. The iron abraded Belle's wrists as she tugged at them, glaring at Silvija. The chains stretched her arms apart and up, just as the leg irons pulled her feet apart. Belle was stretched wide open and vulnerable in her thin, knee-length nightgown. The beast could do anything to her down here.

Belle hissed, "Let me go."

"That's not an option at the moment."

Silvija cranked a lever on the wall, and the chains holding Belle rattled and pulled tight, stretching her arms up and back, until she was almost on her toes. Her ass jutted up, her back curved in.

When she'd brought Belle downstairs, the beast had neglected to put on clothes. In the darkness, illuminated only by Belle's eyesight, she glowed. Her cinnamon skin radiated strength and power, bringing attention to the impressive muscles writhing just beneath. Against her will, Belle became very aware of the high breasts and their hard, crowning nipples. Her arcing ribs and taut belly slid away beneath them. The curved hips, bushy mound, sturdy thighs and legs all proclaimed her strength. This was not a delicate woman.

Belle knew that she might have gone too far in the bed with Silvija, but she would never admit it to the beast, not even if that was the reason she had her tied up like a slave in this damn dungeon. But the beast had made her angry. She had taken her toy. She had taken her life and was forcing her to a place she didn't want to go.

"Is this about that stupid girl?" When Belle didn't answer, Silvija's mouth twisted. "She's not worth it."

"She was worth it to me."

"Worth what? A quick fuck. Or a 'fuck you' to me?" She sneered again. "Either way, trust me, it wasn't. Your rebellion is pointless. You're just going to hurt yourself in the process and make yourself look foolish."

"You mean that you're going to hurt me and make me look foolish."

Silvija smiled coolly. "Whichever." The beast was furious, her anger simmering just beneath the surface of her skin like human heat.

"Let me go, Silvija."

"No. You obviously cannot handle freedom."

Belle growled. "Listen to me, bitch." She rattled the chains imprisoning her arms. "Let me the fuck out of these chains."

"Or what?"

"Is that what you want?" Belle rattled the chains again. "For me to threaten you?"

"No, that's not what I want. But that's been what you've been doing since I met you. Empty threats and provocations that have only managed to completely piss me off." She stalked back and forth in front of Belle, watching her, then looking away. With each provoking word that Belle uttered she grew closer until each motion she made in front of Belle left a slight breeze.

"This is pointless," Belle said, finally calming down. "Let me go."

"Why? Is it because you don't like being under someone else's control? Or because you don't like being under my control?"

"You don't control me, bitch."

"What did I tell you that first day?" She didn't wait for Belle to answer. "This is my clan. Julia bit you. She is my clan, so you are my clan. You are *all* under my protection."

"Do you just get off on this power trip? Is this the only way you can really control your women? To bring them down here and torture them, make them bleed? This is obviously the only way you can think of to control me."

Silvija shot forward suddenly and bunched Belle's nightgown into a shaking fist. "Why do you always take things too far?"

Belle spat in her face. Silvija's eyes flashed. She moved back abruptly, taking pieces of Belle's nightgown with her. Cool air washed over Belle's skin. Silvija deliberately wiped the spit from her face with the bits of her nightgown. Her face was granite hard, and cold.

"Is that how you want to play it?" Silvija's eyes flickered over Belle's face and body, missing nothing, not her rebellious look, not the scornful twist of her mouth, and certainly not the contempt blazing from her eyes. Pieces of Belle's split nightgown hung limply off her shoulders and hips. One shrug and those bits would fall to the floor, leaving her completely naked. A false breath shuddered in her throat, and she felt her breasts move, her nipples harden standing up in the cool air.

"You may not understand yourself now, but I know. You want something from me, puppy. I'm assuming that you find it hard to ask for, but that's all right. I'll give it to you anyway." The cool eyes licked over her again. "But only this once. Next time, next time," her voice was gravelly and thick, "next time, you'll have to beg me for it."

Silvija walked slowly around Belle, taking her time stirring up the prickles of awareness on the bound woman's skin. The air stilled when she stopped behind her. Belle didn't give her the satisfaction of twisting her head around to see what Silvija was doing. She would be stoic. She would wait for whatever the beast thought would move her. Belle steeled herself against the pain that was sure to come.

A whisper of sensation seared down her back. Her skin flinched from it, but the touch was surprisingly gentle. It remained steady and light, threading down the valley of her spine, licking over the rise of her ass, before flaring back up to her shoulder blades. Hands moved through the air, leaving a slight breeze in their wake. The breeze brushed the sensitive skin over her ass, then the hands themselves, shaping the rounded flesh, cupped her. Fingers glided down the backs of her thighs and calves. The beginnings of arousal flared under her skin and spread quickly. She shivered.

Stretched as she was, her body anticipating the sting of pain, the gentle sensation was jarring. And much worse. She ground her teeth together and pulled at the manacles holding her arms captive. That pain grounded her, reminding her why she was here. This pleasure wasn't real. It was poisonous. As much as the source of it was.

"Stop it."

But Silvija didn't stop. The fingers brushed between Belle's thighs, avoiding her intimate place. Then disappeared. The breeze came again when Silvija stood up. She didn't speak. Belle breathed a sigh of relief, but it came too soon. The beast's fingers came back. This time they flickered out to stroke her belly from behind. Belle slammed her head, hoping to catch the beast in the face, but Silvija's was lower. Deliberate breath tingled at the small of her back.

"Fuck you," Belle ground out between her teeth.

The fingers danced over the muscles stretched tight in her stomach, over the flare of ribs, then up to the sensitive underside of her breasts. Sensation writhed in her belly. Hands cupped her breasts, stroked the heavy globes. Belle looked down and saw, to her shame, her nipples plumping up in Silvija's hands, hard and ripe, mere millimetres from the stroking fingers. She felt the beast's tongue on the small of her back. The tongue dipped lower, then teeth scraped the tender skin at the top of her ass as fingers brushed her nipples. A noise escaped Belle. The fingers tugged and flicked her nipples while Silvija bit her from behind. Belle's mind deserted her. Her hips pushed against the air. She pulled against the manacles, scraping her wrists. Words came from behind her, words muffled by the press of skin, sinking into her, incomprehensible but arousing, stoking the flames of her desire.

"No." No. No. No. She couldn't want this humiliation. But the movement of her hips proved her wrong. She didn't know whether she fought against the manacles to kill Silvija or to touch her in return. "No …"

The fingers and tongue disappeared. Belle was breathing heavily but couldn't stop herself. When she opened her eyes—when had she closed them?—Silvija stood in front of her. The beast's eyes were heavy-lidded and savage. It seemed then that the lesson was over, but Silvija reached out. Her hands snagged in Belle's hair and pulled her head back. She buried her face in Belle's throat just as her hand grabbed the out-thrust ass and pulled it close. Silvija's thigh pushed between hers, slid against the shame of her desire. Her pussy wept. The big thigh muscle smoothly stroked her, abraded the delicate flesh of her exposed cunt lips and her clit. The echoes of their fucking sounded loudly in the room.

She would not shame herself by begging, but she was so close to it. So close. Silvija licked her throat, nuzzled her, while her thigh worked against Belle. The heated clove scent of her was overwhelming. Their bodies together seemed to generate another kind of heat, different from the kind exuded when they were piled together in sleep. This heat blossomed under Belle's skin like the sun, incinerating, smouldering. She cried out.

That sound woke Silvija from the trance she had fallen into. The beast moved away from her throat and down Belle's body. The loss of that heat made her want to shout out in pain. This was too much. She tugged harder at the manacles, curling her fingers together so they could slip past the iron. Blood began to seep down her wrists.

Silvija's nose burrowed into the curls at the tops of her thighs. She inhaled deeply and whispered something, something that Belle wasn't meant to hear. But she did.

"So sweet," Silvija said in wonder, "so sweet." Then she took Belle's clit in her mouth. Her world imploded. That's what it felt like as Silvija sucked on her flesh like it was the most delicious thing she'd ever had in her mouth. Belle gasped and her knees went weak. She stumbled against Silvija, and the beast pushed her back upright without relieving her of the blissful torture of her mouth. Belle's hands and fingers scraped against the iron manacles as they finally slid free. Her own blood smell threatened to suffocate her, to drown her deeper in forced pleasure and pain. Belle's hands were raw and bleeding, but she wanted them all over Silvija.

She fell, pushing the tall beast from between her legs, flat against the dirty floor. Silvija grunted and dragged Belle beneath her, pinning her shackled body beneath her superior weight. Her flesh was so hot. The beast's naked belly and breasts pressed into hers. Belle did the only thing that seemed right; she grabbed the beast's face and kissed her.

Silvija tasted of wildness and a wind-tossed sea. Belle's senses revelled, disbelieving in the untamed thing over her. Silvija didn't fight her mouth, she fought for it, biting at Belle's lips, forcing them apart to plunder the tender pink flesh within. Belle bit her back. Their blood melded until they were both drunk on each other and writhing on the floor. Why did she taste so good?

Silvija abruptly pulled her up with a grunt and followed Belle's body with her own. Belle's bare bottom skimmed across the floor and her thighs strained from the awkward position of being pushed flat on the floor with her legs still shackled. Silvija pulled her back to her knees and thrust her fingers deeply inside her.

Belle staggered, but she held on to Silvija's face, catching her fingers in the multitude of plaits, pulling harder against her ravenous mouth. It didn't make sense that she wanted the beast so much. The fingers moved inside her, fucking her with firm, deep strokes. She gasped her delight in Silvija's mouth, telling with her nimble tongue how much she loved her fingers inside, how the trembling in her thighs was a good thing, how fantastic it was to feel her world exploding.

She died again. And it was better than the first time. She clutched at Silvija and let sensation take her away. Belle panted in the beast's arms, trembling in the aftermath of her orgasm. Silvija gently lifted her up, then laid her on the floor. The rough concrete scraped her cheek and palms. Dust and dirt billowed up with each uncontrolled exhalation of her breath. She squeezed her eyes shut. The manacles tugged at her ankles, but she barely felt them.

Silvija stood up and scrubbed her hand over her hair before looking down at Belle. Something in Belle's eyes made her back away toward the stairs. If Silvija had hurt her, it would have been better. It would have made sense for her to flare up in anger and smash everything that Silvija was into the dirty floor beneath her feet. But she hadn't. Her body still throbbed with satisfaction, and her mouth was full of the taste of Silvija.

The beast stood naked at the bottom of the stairs with Belle's bloody handprints streaked across her face. She blinked once, twice, then regained her composure. "I can make your body do anything that I want," she said. "Anything. And don't you ever forget it."

And she left her. Belle blinked at the disappearing figure through the flickering haze of her hatred and lust.

Homeland

Kristyn Dunnion

"That's some pretty fake ID you got there, Squeegee." Terminator Dyke slaps it back in my hand. She crosses her arms over huge, unleashed tits. "Not a chance you're drinking in this establishment."

"Come on, man," I say. "I gotta meet my friend."

"Well, you can meet your friend down at daycare 'til you're old enough to be here legally." The Asshole Lesbians in line behind me all start to snicker. I take a step back. I smile a goofy, shrugging, what-can-I-do kind of smile. Goes over pretty good with the ladies. Even with this style-less idiot, in desperate need of a support bra. I wouldn't be scared to fucking pop her one right on the mouth for patronizing me. It's just I haven't completely given up hope on getting in. I'm broke, and the way I see it, there's purses and pockets to be picked, drinks to be nicked, and lots of Lesbos just waiting to be had. I got work to do tonight, and fighting Quasimodo won't help one bit. I saunter away, lean against the next building, light a smoke. I flip the collar on my customized jean jacket. I give the whole eager lesbian lineup my profile. Very James Dean. Me, leaning poetic under the streetlight on a gloomy night. Young and punk and lonely.

I fondle my most prized possessions in my pocket. You know, those tiny things you keep close by, for luck. A smooth black pebble from the island—that otherworldly wilderness I call home—and the dented, tarnished ring my old lady whipped across the room in that final ugly blowout. I stashed my knapsack in a locker down at the bus station earlier. Nothing freaks a Nice Lesbian Bar like when you show up with a big greasy pack and weeks of travel reeking out of your clothes.

So I pose and smoke in my steel-toed, fourteen-hole shitkickers, army pants, favourite jacket with the *Fuck Shit Up!* hand-painted logo on the back, and my fully erect five inch Mohawk. I take cool, sidelong glances at all these shorthaired women waiting, witness to my alienation. They all have proper ID, of course, and most of them look thirty or something, so it's not like they even need it. Not a punk among them. Just yuppie squares. Comatose, clean professionals. Squash-playing, slacks-wearing, martini-drinking Lesbian Zombies. Half dead, desperate for a rush, and they don't even know it.

My feet ache. The line moves at a pretty good clip so I decide it's all right to have a seat on the stoop, just hunker down and stretch out. When I was real young I used to think I could bounce in and out of Nice Lesbian Bars, city to city, find womanly understanding, Lady Love, shelter. One stop shopping. *Mama.* Took me a while to stop looking for it, hoping. I wonder at that strange phenomenon all across North America: universally bad music, overpriced drinks, mean women, and hostile security. Top four reasons why I take my trade to the Nice Lesbian Bars and my party to the dirty, run-down punk bars. Sick truth is, they sense the sham. Forensic evidence of my rage, my violent scorn for every last one of them piles up unstoppable, and it draws the whiny victims forward, moths to the flame.

Someone has to fall for it. Someone always does. Someone just has to want me.

I see one giving me the eye. She's about 5'7", late twenties, trendy blonde-streaked hair, bone-crunchingly thin with a long nose and a small off-centre mouth. She's wearing some straight pleather clubwear, cream-coloured jacket, low-slung pants, heeled sandals. She tucks her car keys in her purse, laughs nervously with her ugly friends, and looks over her shoulder at me. I give her the spine-tingling, lonely stare-down. Hold her attention for a long minute, then look away. Disdain.

I got a nose for the masochistic type. The rich masochistic type. Perfect for hustlers like me. They usually got a scattered look about them. The kind of woman that only fucks when she's loaded and has secret obsessions even her friends don't know about. An emotional junkie. Loves chaos and conflict 'cause it screws up the chronic order and control she exerts on all material objects in her path. She'll do anything to feed her infinite insecurity, her deeply seated psychic wounds. *Daddy.* The less available you are, the more she'll want you. Especially a no-good, mercenary predator like myself.

When I look back, Blondie's gaping like a trout. All hands dying on deck. I give her a meaningful stare, the shrugging smile. Her part of the line moves forward. They're the next to be let in. She says to her friends, "I forgot something in the car. I'll meet you inside, promise." She bites her lip, fumbles with the keys again and walks this way, peering through her bangs at me. Her friends gesture, make drunken noises, but they turn to go in. When the door swings open, loud dance music pumps out onto the street all around us. Quasimodo, the braless wonder, looks at me and shakes her head.

Blondie drags her left shoe across the sidewalk a little bit with each step. I hate that. She slows as she nears me, eyes trained on the ground, perfectly unsure. Perfect. I will her to look up when she's closing in and she does. Bingo. My best sad face, my very best down-trodden, hard-on-my–luck expression, complete with slight pouting of the lower lip. Eyes clear, with a slight glimmer of hope.

Needless to say it works like lube in a tight hole. She says, "Hi," and mentions the imaginary thing she forgot in the car. I offer to walk her, "beautiful lady alone in the night," and so on. I light a cigarette, give it to her. She pretends to smoke it. I ask about the city we're in, first time passing through, leaving tomorrow, and my only friend has stood me up. Left me stranded.

This causes her concern. "Where will you sleep?"

"Oh, maybe a park or something. Know any good ones?" I say casually, and flatter her into thinking she might be street savvy enough to know what makes a place good to sleep in or not. Her pulse thrums in her tiny neck. I want to snap it. Her skin is pale, dry. She's carefully made up, you can tell at close range, so that she'll look natural from a distance. Clever.

"Why d'ya cover up your freckles?" I say.

"What?" She laughs self-consciously.

"No, serious. I love freckles. They're sexy."

She flushes, pleased with the compliment packed carefully in a crate of criticism. I'm on the make. She's sipping juice from a bottle, offers me some, and I swig it back. She's saying something about the juice, but I'm swallowing so I can't hear. She lifts her hand in protest, squawks out loud, but I drain the bottle in one long gulp and toss it away, into the street. I'm taking her for every thing she's got. She giggles.

We get to the car and, whaddayaknow, the "thing" she's looking for isn't there! I say, "How sad I won't get to see this city while I'm here." She looks at me sideways in that profound, fateful moment when she makes her decision, and voila, we're in her brand-new, candy-apple red Honda Civic hatchback that Daddy gave her. The tinted windows whirl down, the music blares, and we're off. She gives me a tour of her favourite American-owned coffee retailers, the shopping mall where she bought her ridiculous outfit, her hairstylists' shop ("He's really cool and sooo sweet"). She points out the CN Tower with its rotating restaurant in the fat bulge of it, the glass elevators on the side sliding up, sliding down. She claims it's the tallest in the city, in the country, in the world, practically. I shrug.

She rests her hand on my knee at a stoplight. She leans toward me. "You and me, we're going to fuck tonight."

I smile wide and the knot inside tightens. I say, "Is that so?" and she nods her head yes. She's got that terrible smugness about her, like the way cowards ego-bloat when they're high on cocaine. She tells me I'm hot.

Someone honks. The light is already green, and she stalls the car. More honks. Her tires squeal. She drives nervously, hopping from one lane to another, making bad decisions, going nowhere. She speeds up to make a yellow light then slams on the breaks, sliding us halfway into the intersection, and I think I might not even get a chance to kill this bitch, she might do us both in first!

"Smoke?" I offer her a joint. She refuses, saying she usually likes coke or speed or crystal meth or like any club drug, really, but definitely not pot 'cause it makes her all …

"Paranoid?" I say quietly.

"Um, yeah. I guess." She asks, "Wanna see the lake?" and I say, "Sure, why not. I like nature. Water."

Her hand is back on my thigh now, she's scratching at me with her long manicured nails. She says, "Just looking at you gets me wet," and I think, how original, you stupid, boring broad. She says something about some fantasy on the beach. The one where a stranger takes her down and frees her from herself; she lets loose, wild and dirty, leaves her endless petty hang-ups behind. I'm thinking how easy it'd be to stash her body, take the car, hit the highway. And then she's swinging sharply to the left, careening across three lanes of traffic, narrowly making it to the on-ramp for a decrepit express lane going in a completely different direction.

"You seem a little wired," I say, clutching my seatbelt, snapping it into place, knocking her hand off of me.

"Yeah," she hiccups. "The pills I took are kinda kicking in." She laughs; there's a maniacal twinge to her face now, and it looks eerie in the silver lights along the highway.

I lick my lips. "Why don't we pull over right now?" I say, like I've said to a million other creeps who have driven me around. "Ever done it on the side of the road?"

She giggles. She's undoing her shirt buttons, steering one-handed. I look out the window and can't read any signs. The letters are blurred. I squint. Doesn't help. I can't read a single word in print. I have no idea where we're headed and I feel woozy. Weird. I open the window a crack because it's hot, and every-thing's too close. I want out. Wish I had convinced her to ditch the car. We're speeding along even faster, it seems, although cars are honking, passing on the left. Lights blur. She turns up the music. Electronic, trancey, house shit. It starts to make sense to me, for once.

A car pulls up and keeps pace beside us. Dudes are hanging out the back windows yelling "Show us your dyke tits!" She laughs and shakes her shirt the rest of the way undone. They scream and honk, peel past us, and when they drive away I can see two bare asses in their back window.

We hit gravel and she jerks the wheel sharply. We're back on the road.

"Hey," I say.

Numbness spreads through my limbs. I take deep breaths; the sensation matures, becomes solid in my chest. It beats outward with each pumping thrust of my heart valve, fast and furious. My skin is hot; it is paper igniting. It is kindling. It crackles. Flames leap to my fingertips as they trace a delicate dance around my cheeks, down my neck, back to my mouth. I'm so thirsty.

"Waaater?" I say thickly.

She produces a sparkly bottle; her smile wavers crooked like Charlie Brown's T-shirt. The bottle is blue and light and cool and so out of reach. The car seats are miles apart now. I can't move my arm, but somehow the bottle is there, in my hand. I can't feel it. Liquid splooshes out the top, shocks my face, runs down my shirt. The tip of my tongue taps around on skin, sucks up the coveted drops.

So thirsty. My large tongue, ungainly in my mouth.

She laughs and bounces in her seat, mouth open, singing along all party-circuit mode, like she's in one of those fucking car ads. I try to say something, yell. Nothing comes out. There's a low sound (a bear?) growling (me?). I want her to stop this, stop the car, pull over, and end it.

She faces me, head swivels on her skeletron neck, says, "The Juice, it was in the Juice," and her face chainsaws apart into huge mawing gaps. "Liquid K for me'n'allmyfriends."

I pull the seatbelt, but can't move. Trapped. Only my eyes work. I pinprick gaze a falling star, a million miles away, one that I will never reach. My hand rests immobile on my pocket, in my lap. I close my eyes. Fireworks trail inside the lids, red lines spiral and drip, invade the velvet deep. I open them and things are much, much worse.

The truck is upon us, blasting the horn. The driver is screaming, waving his hands, and Blondie is smiling, hands up, eyes closed, head back like she's about to come. I'm thinking, shit, now I'll never make any money tonight. Metal grid pounds into the Civic's hood, grinds slow motion through the crumpled car, legs buckle and cramp, the ripping sound fills my ears. I'm looking down into my lap at one hand. My other hand is still on the armrest, and it is an acrobat, flying through the air at a tremendous speed, far away from me.

There is the suddenness. The explosion. There is brightness and lightness, the dull roaring rage that consumes me. There's the smooth black pebble in my pocket, from my homeland.

In Circles

Aurelia T. Evans

He did not run out or slam the door or shout at her. There was the snick of the door latch and then she could hear his Chevy rumble out of the parking space. Her apartment smelled of Alfredo sauce, cat dander, and the detergent he used on his dress shirts. He left his wine glass on the coffee table next to his Blackberry. She would have to mail it to him. He would not want to come back.

Her breathing seemed loud and her skin warm as she pulled the open sides of her blouse over her breasts. Reaching down, she pulled her panties up over her thighs and rescued her jeans from the armchair. She tried to be as calm as possible as she brought their wine glasses to the sink. Their bases rattled together, and she almost dropped one. She rinsed them out and put them on the counter. Still holding her jeans over her left elbow, she padded down the hall to her room. The ivory sheets were turned down. She threw her jeans into the laundry basket and went into the bathroom for her pills. Her fingers struggled with the childproof lid before she could finally get the bottle open. She took out one tiny pill and swallowed it dry. Her face contorted against its sharp bitterness, and she caught the contortion in the mirror, seeing the person that Daniel left.

"Plain Kate, and bonny Kate, and sometimes Kate the curst,

but Kate, the prettiest Kate in Christendom." These were the words that wooed her. He whispered them again in her ear tonight, knowing how she liked it. Whispered them with every pearly button he slid out of its hole as he kissed down her sternum to the valley between her breasts. She did not wear a bra. She liked the firmness and weight of him over her and her legs wrapped around his, on the sofa like teenagers. Except as a teenager, she had never done anything like this. It was hedonistic and heady, and her skin was a furnace. All her worries sparkled on the back of her tongue with the wine. She kissed him as she unbuttoned her jeans. He helped her pull them down her legs. He always liked her strong legs. Her stomach fluttered as his fingertips slid up her newly shaved legs, and she thought for a moment about closing her legs again, crossing them. But she was thirty-three and horny and a little drunk. She forgot just a few seconds too late.

He had stopped with her panties caught at her knees. Stared. Between her legs, then up at her face, stared at the dilated horror in her eyes. His face changed colour as his emotions ran over it like water: confusion, revelation, disgust, betrayal, and revulsion. He stood up, grabbed his jacket and briefcase, fastened his trousers, and left.

Daniel Foreman was her second boyfriend. After a year and a half of patience, Kate wanted to unveil. Daniel was a nice man. Her thoughts had skipped through each of the key phrases in her books: diversity, body image, positive thinking, love yourself, relativity. He thought her pretty, and that was more than she ever expected. They were adults, they were in love, they had been talking about engagement.

Some boundaries, Kate thought as she stared into the mirror, are meant to be crossed. He had never given her a ring. At least he did not find out on their wedding night. And that's when the tears started. She shrugged the rose-coloured blouse off her shoulders, standing there in her underwear with her throat swollen and her eyes turning red. Broad shoulders, flat breasts, and purple stretch marks on her stomach. She had good skin when it was clear, and she used moisturizers and exfoliated; she shaved everywhere.

Grabbing a handful of tissues, she wiped her dripping nose, trying not to make a sound. Who she was hiding from?—it was just her and the cat in the apartment. All she knew was that she did not want to cry now. Before getting into the shower, she lit a few scented candles and shut off the lights. She could see enough. Everything looked better by candlelight. She slipped behind the shower curtain. She jerked the knob to the left until the water burned her, then shifted it back to the right, and it cooled down slightly.

The last time she really looked in the mirror properly was at her best friend Judy's tenth birthday party. Judy had a sleepover with three other girls, and they sat in the Jacuzzi tub with their bathing suits on, giggling in the bubbles. Kate wore shorts over her bathing suit because without them you could see. Eventually, the discussion turned to ghost stories, and Judy retrieved a book from her bookshelf and started reading from it in a low, intense voice. The hook, the babysitter's call, the long fingernails, Mary Worth—all the classics.

"They have stories about Bloody Mary all over the world," Judy whispered. "She's always in the mirror after you chant her name, dripping in blood, reaching out to grab you. If you don't turn on the lights in time, they never find your remains."

Judy set the book down and looked at all of her friends huddled in the tub. Then she smiled. "Wanna try it?" she said.

Candlelight, locked doors, fluffy white towels around their shoulders, they stared into the mirror and chanted Bloody Mary, turning in circles five times for each name.

"Bloody Mary, Bloody Mary, Bloody Mary, Bloody Mary."

The girls all looked at each other and tittered nervously. Finally, one of them found the courage to turn once more, so the rest of them did too. "Bloody Mary."

They all peered into the mirror, half wanting to shield their eyes and half wanting to see the fruits of their spell. Kate did not know which one of them screamed first. But once one screamed, they all started screaming, stampeding to the door, unlocking it, and yanking it open. It was not until they were in the master bedroom that it occurred to Judy to just turn on the bathroom light. It went without saying that there was nothing in the bathroom, nothing in the mirror but reflections of sheepish smiles. Two of them swore they had seen something in the mirror—a person behind them, a face. Kate had not seen anything. Still, all of them slept tightly huddled together in their sleeping bags, with a night light on in the hall. Maybe there had been something in that mirror. But like all nights, it dissolved into morning. That was when things were relatively normal, when she still had dreams of flowers blossoming, ugly ducklings turning into swans, beasts into beauties.

Kate let the hot water pound against her back as she squeezed vanilla body wash onto her loofah. Her eyes felt swollen shut, and she could barely see, but she knew her body by touch as well as by sight. The soap smoothed over her arms, then her stomach and back, then down her legs. Hesitating, she curled the loofah between her legs. She thought she could feel it. A little less than an inch wide, a little more than an inch long. It was disgusting. It was there. She jerked her hand away and turned into the spray again.

It had been Judy who first saw her—Kate's daring attempt to change in the girls' locker room after seventh grade gym. She was not the only girl who preferred to change in the bathroom stalls, but they were all girls there, right? Looking was never supposed to be a problem as long as no one *really* looked. But when Judy caught a glimpse, she couldn't help but stare. Kate's face flushed bright red, and she rushed to cover herself. She felt like she was going to vomit at the look of confusion and disgust on Judy's face. Kate was lucky that Judy didn't spread the word to the entire school. Instead, their friendship waned until it was nothing but awkward glances in the hallways. Middle school was not a bastion of nonconformity, and Kate went back to changing in the bathroom stalls all the way through high school.

She turned off the water and reached for a towel. She dried the same way she cleaned. A brief swipe between her legs, and she looked into the mirror. It was crooked. She blinked, reached up to set it right on its nail. The corner cut into her finger. She hissed between her teeth, bringing her finger to her mouth to suck on it. In the fogged glass and candlelight, she could see the blur of deep purple that was her towel and the lighter tan that was her body.

For a moment, her breath shuddered the candlelight, and it looked like there was someone behind her. She turned around, but there was no one there. She felt that queer tension in her lower back, the one she got when it was too quiet and she had strange ideas. Her fingers fumbled with the light switch and flicked it on quickly. The light changed everything. She could breathe. And she did not have to look. She swung the bathroom door almost closed on her way out. Those turned-down sheets whispered under the weight of one body. Kate kept the lamp on, curled under the covers with her arms around a pillow. There was a steady ringing in her left ear, and she thought she heard her cat, Gracie, in the bathroom. With her eyes shut she saw Daniel's face dissolve into the lightning in her eyelids.

Dinner by herself the next night did not seem so dire as long as she kept the television on. Gracie sat in the hall with the tip of her tail twitching irritably and watched Kate eat her ready-made lasagna. She lost herself in the motion of the fork from her plate to her mouth and in the news story that kept coming up on every station. For the last five weeks, all of the local and some of the national stations had been covering the Chicago serial murders. Three women brutally killed in their own homes—all single, their houses untouched but for their mutilated bodies, and no leads. All suspects in custody released. Little physical evidence. No comment. The new story, though, was about another woman, same M.O. But this woman was alive.

The reporter looked gravely into the camera. His voice was sincere and impartial. Kate felt nauseated as she watched the newscast show fuzzy photos of the crime scene. "Last night, a woman was brutally attacked in her one-bedroom apartment at Highway 70 and Belgium Street. Neighbours claimed they heard screaming, and one couple called the police. Upon arriving, the police found her on her bathroom floor. They transported her to St. Bethany's Medical Center, where she stayed in critical condition until this afternoon. The doctors are confident she will recover. The police believe that this was the work of the serial killer they're calling the Surgeon."

The report cut from the news desk to a Hispanic woman from the victim's apartment complex with her three-year-old daughter propped on her hip. "We're keeping everything locked, but I wish we had bars on the windows, you know? What else can we do?"

The camera cut to a business woman on the street. "My friends and I are terrified. We try not to stay out too late, and we don't go home alone. But that doesn't really help, does it? This guy gets these women *in their homes*. It's horrible."

Cut back to the reporter. "As is typical for the Surgeon, there was no forced entry, and the police could find no physical evidence on the scene. An anonymous tip from the police department stated that all four women share a similar medical condition, but that the specific details are being withheld. More on this breaking story as it develops."

Because she worked at St. Bethany's Kate knew a little more than the reporters, although she was not supposed to. Lila, a nurse from Emergency, came by at the end of Kate's shift as a receptionist in Psychiatrics, dying to tell somebody.

White female, late thirties, no allergies, acute blood loss, lacerations all over her body with particular attention paid to the stomach, the face, and the breasts. The wounds were too cleanly cut and too particular to be the work of an amateur. The first few articles called the killer the Plastic Surgeon because of his skill and the focus of his attentions, but the pseudonym was eventually shortened to the Surgeon. After all, the killer wasn't putting anything into them. He was taking things out.

"You wouldn't believe it," Lila said, sitting on the bench across from the bathroom sinks. "I mean, the others pretty much went straight to the morgue. This one's strong; blood pressure's finally stable after transfusions, although she's still unconscious. We don't know if there was any brain damage, but let me tell you, there's *going* to be brain damage if she wakes up. Jesus Christ." Her voice was filled with that sickly combination of both eagerness and contempt. "That's one psycho bastard, whoever he is. Her face is going to be a mess. He took her lips. And he cut off her breasts. He practically gutted her—one of her kidneys is missing. It's like fucking Charles Manson or Hannibal Lector or something."

"Lila, I'm about to go home and have dinner," Kate said. "Do you have to tell me every last detail?"

"Believe me, you haven't heard anything yet," Lila replied. "You know, it was one thing when he killed these women. That was horrible. But I never really thought about what would happen if they, you know, lived. Skin grafts are only going to be able to do so much. Imagine if you had to look in the mirror every day and see that for the rest of your life."

Kate slung her purse over her shoulder. "Yeah," she murmured. "Look, I deal with mentally sick people all day. Do I have to take it home with me?"

"Just thought you'd want to know," Lila said, shrugging. "Anything happening next weekend? Want to go see a movie or something? Anything but a slasher film."

"I think I'll stay in," Kate replied.

"What else is new? Hey," Lila called as Kate headed out, "lock your doors, okay?"

Kate stopped eating when the crime shows started to come on. She wasn't hungry anymore. She took out some Saran wrap, covered the rest of the lasagna, and threw the leftovers into the freezer. Cooking for one, her freezer always seemed to be full. She changed the channel to something more palatable than corpses and criminals (wasn't reality terrible enough?) and turned the sound down. It was enough to have the mumble of voices in the emptiness. She just stood in her living area, not really watching the screen. Usually, at this time of night she would call Daniel or her mother and talk until ten. But calling Daniel was no longer an option. Her mother knew she had been dating, and Kate didn't want to answer any questions. Kate's silence would be her mother's answer.

She remembered the talks in her childhood bedroom. Her mother would blame herself—she told the doctors no to surgery when Kate was about three months old and the problem began to surface. Kate's mother finally brought up the possibility of cosmetic adjustment when Kate was fourteen and beginning to weed: growing bone, growing breasts, growing hair. Kate remembered that she jumped on the idea, but her mother balked when actually confronted with the possibility. In retrospect, Kate supposed that the prospect of rendering Diana Barrett's only daughter practically sterile convinced her otherwise. Kate might have had it done herself, but she tended to live paycheque to paycheque. Also, it was embarrassing enough to go to a gynecologist once every two years (she refused to go more often); she felt her tongue twist at the thought of calling her insurance company and asking whether genital corrective surgery was covered.

She turned the clock radio to the soft-rock station and kept the volume low so that the distant sound of the television and the crooning from the radio mingled into mindlessness. White noise. She did not bother turning down the covers to her bed. She sat on the comforter and cushioned her back with her pillow before opening her book to its first page.

She caught herself falling asleep over the pages more than once. Gracie had deigned to join her on the bed, curled between Kate's knees like it was her own little nest. At 9:48 p.m., according to the digital clock, Gracie leapt off the bed and ran into the bathroom with her tail high like a flag. She sometimes did that when Kate opened a can of sardines or when a stranger came into the house and Gracie would flee under the bed. Kate didn't think anything of it until the yowling started. It was unlike anything Kate ever heard from her cat before—low, round, and resonant—too loud to be coming from Gracie's slight body.

Setting the book on the nightstand, Kate made her way to the bathroom and pushed the door open. The lamplight from her bedroom spilled into the narrow room. One of her candles was also burning on the counter. She could not remember lighting it. Kate saw Gracie's silhouette and was about to flip on the lights when she saw the reflection of a dark figure in the room. Her head jerked to the right. Nobody was there.

She looked back to the mirror. The dark figure was still there, in the shadows from the glare of the light. Kate's eyes shifted from reflection to nothing and back again. Panic and confusion tightened her chest, and her hand froze above the light switch. Each second lasted minutes, but flew. She was suddenly nine years old, feeling superstition accompanied by terror and its thrill.

A sound. She did not want to look away from the figure, but the sound distracted her briefly. Enough to see that Gracie was lapping at a trickle of dark liquid that ran down the side of the mirror. One thick line, almost black. Movement caught her eyes, and Kate watched as the figure moved forward, not into the light from the bedroom but into the light of the candle. Sodden clumps of hair framed a thin face and body. That was all that Kate saw before she reeled back and shot out of the bathroom. She was running into the parking lot outside before she realized that she had left her purse, keys, and phone back in the apartment. She whirled around, looking for someone who might let her use their phone. But it was not a safe neighbourhood, and Kate realized she did not know any of her neighbours.

She dropped onto the curb and hugged her knees, looking at her front door. She needed to go in. She needed something. She could not leave with nothing. Her thin silver watch clicked slower than her pulse, and ten minutes passed before she could move. Did she see a figure or did she create the figure? Was she just tired, jumping at shadows because of the news? She was probably in more danger in the parking lot than in her own apartment. Glancing around, she made her way back into the building. Kate shut the door behind her but didn't lock it, leaving herself an easy exit.

Gracie was sitting on the couch, licking her paws as though nothing had happened. The normalcy soothed Kate. Because Gracie was usually terrified of strangers, then surely there were no strangers here. But she grabbed a kitchen knife anyway, holding it defensively as she edged back into her bedroom. The bathroom door was still half open, the candle still flickering. For a moment, Kate saw nothing in the mirror. She crept into the bathroom, raising her knife and looking into every corner. There was nothing but the line of dried liquid on the mirror, the sway of the curtains, and the dark mass of her towels hanging on the wall.

And then the bathroom door slammed behind her. She screamed and almost dropped the knife. Her free hand clutched at the knob, slipped in sweat, but the knob refused to budge. Kate looked up into the mirror and the figure was there again, peering at her over her shoulder.

In the darkness Kate could see the figure more clearly. Her clothing was nondescript, ankle- and wrist-length, soaked and stained. She was thin. But everything paled beside the blood, black in the candlelight. There were gouges in the woman's face, bald patches where hair used to be, and blood trickled like tears, cutting through the tacky clots and knotting beneath the wounds. The woman's eyes were bright and glistened wetly in the mirror.

There was a tap, tap, tap, tap, and Kate could not tear her eyes away to notice that her hand was shaking so violently that the knife was tapping against the sink counter.

The woman cocked her head to the side. Her face was expressionless, but the gesture made her seem almost compassionate. Some still place in Kate's head thought the woman was almost beautiful. Kate felt a hand in her hair, stroking it lightly.

"I always come when I'm called," the woman in the mirror said. "If only you are patient."

The voice was unremarkable. Kate looked over her shoulder. There was still no one there. But she could *feel* the pressure of fingers on her scalp. The rhythmic stroking and the voice calmed her in spite of herself.

"What do you want?" The words were out of her mouth before Kate even realized that she could speak.

The woman shook her head. "What do *you* want?" she asked.

Kate hissed between her teeth when the pressure on her scalp increased as the woman curled her nails into the flesh and drew down. Kate thought of an apple peeler. A finger traced the side of Kate's face. Kate could see it in the mirror, she could feel it, but it was not there. She tried to move away from the woman's hands, but her feet seemed frozen in place. The woman just leaned with her, her warmth seeping through Kate's clothing.

"Do you want me to leave?" the woman asked, no louder than a whisper. Kate could hear every word, every breath.

"Who…?" Kate could not finish. The woman's nail split her skin from forehead to jaw, and Kate watched the woman smile and bring her finger to her mouth to suck.

"You know who I am," the woman said. Her breath felt clean and cold where blood welled into the furrow lining Kate's cheek. The knife fell to the floor with a clatter, and Kate felt a tongue, wet and hot, slide up the cut along her scalp. The woman pressed her moist lips to Kate's temple where the heartbeat raced.

"Do you want me to leave?" the woman asked. But she seemed to already know the answer.

If she could have, Kate would have worn a scarf close around her face or called in sick the next day. But she did not want to stay at home, and everyone would have asked about the scarf as much as they asked about the cut along the right side of her face. She explained that Gracie got a little crazy and scratched her, but she didn't think most of her co-workers believed her. The cut was too deep and a little too wide for a cat's claws, and repeating Gracie's name in response to concerned queries only reminded her that she'd left the cat alone in the apartment with that woman.

"You look like hell," Lila said, leaning on the receptionist counter and almost toppling a pile of manila folders.

"Thank you."

"No, really," Lila said. "It's not just that cut. You did clean it, right?"

Kate raised an eyebrow. She'd bought hydrogen peroxide on her way to the Holiday Inn, along with a bottle of Simply Sleep. She covered the mirrors in the hotel room with sheets from the other bed and slept with all the lights on. It had taken her an hour in the shower and a cheap hand mirror to make sure that all the blood was out of her hair. In spite of the medicine, she still woke up around 5:30. Unwilling to linger alone, she came to work early.

Even now, she wasn't sure whether it had been a nightmare or a hallucination. She would swear in court that she had seen what she saw and felt what she felt, but if working in a psychiatric ward taught her anything, she knew that what people saw and felt could not always be trusted. She remembered the woman behind her in the mirror. She remembered the nails in her scalp and watching her cheek open like ripe fruit. She remembered the woman's hands heavy on her shoulders then slipping under the slight curve of her breasts as though reluctant to let go while her image faded. She remembered tenderness in the pain. Once the woman disappeared completely, Kate still stood there, in that familiar position, staring at herself in the mirror as black blood trickled down her face.

It took all the strength left in her arms to reach for the bathroom door. It wasn't locked anymore, and the light that spilled in reminded her that there was indeed light in the world. She stumbled out, unaware that she was hyperventilating until her vision blurred and darkened. She rested her head against the doorframe and gathered herself. As soon as she could walk, she ran, grabbing the things she needed this time.

Lila was still looking at her.

"Yes, I cleaned it. I'm not stupid," Kate answered. "Stop staring at me, it's creeping me out. Don't you have work to do or something?"

"That's what I'm doing," Lila said. She pulled a file from under her arm and tossed it on top of Kate's keyboard. "Check out your new patient up here, honey. You won't believe it."

"Marlene Davidson, thirty-seven years old," Kate read, "lacerations, possibly self-inflicted, possible Post Traumatic Stress Disorder … holy shit, this is the woman who—"

"Survived the Surgeon," Lila finished, grinning. "One and the same. Her family isn't letting her talk to the press, but yours truly knows why she's being transferred up here. It's not just to get her away from the public eye and give her counselling to help her adjust."

Kate's eyes sped over the file. And froze when she read the initial doctor's concluding evaluation.

"Yep," Lila said, seeing that she had reached the juiciest information. "She actually said that the Surgeon was Mary Worth. Isn't that just sad? Imagine, Bloody Mary. Did you ever play that game when you were a kid? I was always afraid to try."

What Kate was doing was not permitted. She was neither a nurse nor a doctor; she had no business entering any patient's room unless she had someone else present or there was an emergency. She stood outside the door, her hands gripping her sleeves. Finally, when the coast was clear, Kate unlocked the private room and slipped inside. It was a small room without much in the way of decoration except for flowers in a plastic vase. The bed was propped up, and Marlene was reading a book. Her right hand trembled violently as she turned the page. She looked up at Kate as she came closer and waited for Kate to explain herself, her ragged expression troubled but almost trusting.

"I'm sorry to bother you," Kate murmured. She tried not to stare. She knew that disfigured patients never liked it. But it was hard not to. "I don't mean to …"

Marlene's face immediately changed. "I see. You're here because you think I'm crazy." She had a slight lisp because of her missing lips, but Kate could understand her perfectly.

"No, no, no, nothing like that."

"Or you want to see what she did to me." Marlene's voice was rough and accusing, but underneath was a note of self-deprecation.

"Do you think you're crazy?" Kate asked.

"Bloody fucking Mary nearly killed me. I was there. It's not the sort of thing you just forget." Marlene carefully rested her head against her pillow and exhaled at the ceiling. "Of course I think I'm crazy."

Kate pulled a chair closer to the bed and sat down, hugging Marlene's file to her chest. "Do you … do you mind telling me about it?"

Marlene did not move her head, but her eyes turned to look at Kate. In the midst of her mutilated face, they looked particularly bright blue. Kate was once again struck by the odd thought that the face—like that of the woman in the mirror—was beautiful. Kate's arms pebbled with goosebumps.

"You're not a doctor, are you? You're not even a nurse," Marlene said.

Kate shook her head.

"Why do you want to know?" Marlene asked quietly. "Are you going to run down and tell the damn media every sordid detail?"

"I'm not a plant," Kate said.

"Are you *different*?" There was a sort of nastiness to the question. Kate held the file closer.

"Excuse me?"

"Do you keep secrets?"

"What?"

"Your face," Marlene said. "That cut. She likes them different."

"What are you talking about?" Kate felt herself constrict, pull inward. This was what she had wanted to hear, yet the white-washed walls of the room seemed too close.

"You've looked at my file or else you wouldn't be here. If you didn't notice it the first time, look again. I'm not …" she paused. "… typical. I was born female. I'm still a woman. But I guess some people might not think I am. She likes that." Marlene's voice shook, but not from shame. "She likes the ambiguity because it makes a real difference when she changes us. You know the legend, right? When she was alive, she killed young women and bathed in their blood to stay beautiful."

"That's not the way I heard it. I heard that she killed children after her daughter died," Kate said.

"It's different wherever you go," Marlene said, shaking her head. "She's still killing women. She wants women. But you have to understand something." Marlene bent forward, those bright blue eyes coming closer, her mutilated face filling Kate's vision. Kate wanted to lean away, but the back of her chair kept her from doing so.

"She wants women who will want her back. She has her own little collection of freaks that have kept her here. She may not be alive, but she exists. She's existed all this time. And she can't be stopped."

By now, Marlene's bandaged hand was clutching Kate's wrist, and Kate could see blood seeping through—she must have pulled some stitches. Kate was beginning to think this was a terrible idea. The more she looked at Marlene, the more she looked like Mary.

"You have no idea. But you will. She did that to you, didn't she?" Marlene said.

"It was my cat."

"Bullshit," Marlene spat. "What does she want with you? What's wrong with you? It doesn't matter where you go, she's in the mirrors. Do you see any mirrors in here? No, I told them to take them out. But I still see her, wherever there are reflections. She wants to finish the work done on me. And then she'll get you. There were three other women. You've probably seen them on the news. At least one of them looks like she's different. But we're all women. And that's what she wants from us. Don't you understand? She *wants* women."

"I should go," Kate said, standing and trying to extricate her wrist, but Marlene clutched at her as though she was falling.

"No! You have to listen," Marlene hissed. She twisted in her bed. "She'll make you wish for death. Please, they won't believe me, but you do, don't you? You've seen her. She's touched you. Don't let her fool you. Don't let her take you. She'll kill you like all the others. She takes what makes you a woman. And she emasculates you. *Yes.* You believe me now? How else would I know?"

Kate stopped pulling away. Marlene's grip loosened until it was just her fingertips against the sensitive blue veins on the underside of Kate's wrist. She stared into Marlene's too bright blue eyes. Now she needed to know. She *needed* to know.

"She took my breasts," Marlene said. "She took my lips. She took my face. She took my stomach. She punctured what might have been my uterus in another life. She took my—she sliced into me and took my fallen testes. It doesn't matter what the doctor calls them—that might as well be what they are. It's what I am. Except I'm not that anymore. She took all of me, even the parts I wanted to keep. And I wish she had killed me, but I'm too much of a coward. I'm a monster, but I won't look into a mirror. I spent my life wishing I could cut myself open, but now … I won't let her kill me. I won't."

The doorknob rattled and turned, and Kate jerked around. She could feel her face turning red. Dr. Langley came through with his nurse Cecilia. He looked up from his clipboard in surprise when he saw Kate there.

"Miss Barrett, I didn't know you were in here." He looked between the two women. "I'm sorry, did I interrupt anything?"

"I was just keeping her company," Kate said. Her voice was thin and breathy, but she could not seem to open her throat enough. "Until someone came."

"I hope you weren't bothering her." The doctor looked over his glasses at her, ready to be disapproving.

"She wasn't," Marlene said. "I wanted someone with me.

Someone who would listen." Marlene pulled her hand away from Kate's wrist and looked down into her lap.

"That's what I'm here for," Dr. Langley said with false joviality. "Miss Barrett needs to get back to her work. May I have Miss Davidson's file, please?"

Kate handed Dr. Langley the file. She noticed that there was blood on her wrist from Marlene's earnestness. Dr. Langley's face drew tight in disgust, and Kate hid her hand behind her back. She would wash it thoroughly when she left, but she would be unable to wash the blush of swelling that would eventually bruise.

"Please," Marlene whispered to Kate. "Believe me. Help me."

"I—"

"Miss Barrett." Dr. Langley ushered her out of the room and closed the door emphatically behind her.

Kate stared at the apartment door. It was still mostly light out, and the quiet was broken only by the occasional rush and crunch of a passing car. She peered through the blinds but couldn't see much, mostly the reflection of her own eyes. She recoiled, fearful of what Marlene had said about seeing Mary in every reflection.

Her fingers fumbled with her keys, sliding the jagged edge into the lock and turning. The door opened. Gracie came up to her immediately, demanding to be fed, rubbing against Kate's ankles and meowing as though Kate had never fed her in her life. All the tension seemed to flow out. Nothing happened. Gracie was fine. Marlene was wrong, sick, traumatized. Kate was just exhausted. What had happened was some kind of hallucination because of what had happened with Daniel. As she poured dry food into Gracie's bowl, Kate looked at the Blackberry still sitting on the coffee table.

She wants women. But she wants women who will want her back.

Kate approached the coffee table and picked up the Blackberry. She had first met Daniel in a bar after she got off work, which would have been the last place that Kate would have thought she'd be picked up. But Daniel was a businessman there for the same reason she was, just to unwind, not to get any action. He was sitting next to her during a karaoke contest. He did not even know her when he elbowed her in her ribs, and with that winning smile, told her to take a chance. Kate would never do it, and although Daniel kept goading her, it turned into a talk about how bad some of the contestants were, then about their preferences in music. When Daniel asked whether she wanted to meet him the next evening for dinner, Kate was surprised enough to say yes.

Going out with him was one of the most exhilarating things she had ever done. He made her feel like more than what she saw in the mirror. Until he left. He made her doubt her disgust. Until he recoiled. Then she could see what she had always seen before, know finally that it was utterly untouchable, that *she* was utterly untouchable. Fingertips ghosted over her thighs, and she could almost taste the wine again, hear the door latch. Fingertips over her wrists, blood seeping and smearing onto her skin. Fingertips through her hair and a hot tongue tasting her. It occurred to her that if Mary had really been there, she'd already seen her, all of her. And she'd kissed her anyway.

Kate picked up the Blackberry and opened her cell phone, pressing three to speed dial Daniel. She looked at the television screen—she had not turned it off the night before on her way out, and it was still on the National Geographic Channel, something about the lost city of Atlantis. Kate clicked the television off as she listened to Daniel's landline begin to ring.

Four rings and a click. "Hello?"

"Hi. Daniel?"

There was only the humming of static in her ear.

"You ... um ..."

"I don't want to talk, Kate," Daniel said. "There's not ... I can't ..."

"There's plenty to say," Kate replied. "You just don't want to say it. Besides, I didn't ..."

"You didn't tell me," Daniel interrupted. "You didn't tell me what was wrong. You should've warned me."

Kate sighed, sinking onto her sofa. She felt a tension headache building. "And what was I supposed to say, Daniel? What could I have possibly said that wouldn't have led to the same thing? What part of 'I have a clit that looks like a small penis' would have been remotely attractive to you if just seeing it was enough to make you run?"

There was another long silence. "I deserved to know."

"No, you clearly didn't," Kate snapped. "I have your fucking Blackberry. Do you want to come get it yourself, or do you want me to send it to you?"

"Maybe it's best if you send it to me. I'll mail you a cheque for the shipping charge."

"Don't bother. I'll send it cheap. You may get it within the next three weeks." Kate pushed the button that ended the call. She was shaking again, but only part of it was fear. Another part was anger. It was almost exhilarating. She had never said it out loud to anybody before—only her personal physician, and later the gynecologist, with their comfortably alienating jargon. Her mother always went out of her way to never say exactly what was wrong with her daughter, and Kate took her cue from her mother. And now she'd said it. It was out. Someone knew. And she was okay.

But Marlene wasn't. The thought brought Kate crashing down from the momentary high. Furrows in her face, smooth sewn skin where her lips used to be, skin grafts from her back for the worst places, black threads in her flesh like Frankenstein's monster. Gutted and cut off. Kate just had scratches down her cheek and along the back of her head; Marlene was transformed. Marlene thought that the Surgeon was something as ridiculous and fantastical as Bloody Mary Worth, like a supernatural Jack the Ripper killing freaks instead of whores. Kate did not know what to think. The bathroom mirror drew her damning curiosity, but she did not want to see Mary in the mirror if what happened was real. If what happened was possible. Which it wasn't. But Marlene was in a hospital bed, and she *knew* about Kate. And she looked like Mary.

She wants women who will want her back.

A crack in the mirror, a line of blood down the glass. Her blood.

I always come when I'm called.

She was at her bathroom door before she knew it. The entire space of time between the living area and the bedroom was lost. Her fingers clenched around the brass door knob, tightening in anticipation of whatever was in the room. She had called Mary, and now Mary was calling her—if any of this was real at all. The door opened of its own accord, twisting Kate's arm until the underside of her wrist was exposed. Fingerprints and bloodstains.

The candle was still flickering deep in its wax, the wick almost burnt through. Invisible hands cupped her face and drew her into sight of the mirror. The door closed behind her. Breath ghosted over mouth until full lips pressed against hers, and Kate could see Mary's head in the mirror covering her face—everything seemed like a surreal dream.

"You met my dear Marlene," Mary murmured. Kate could feel each word on her mouth; her tongue licked them away as Mary moved behind her. "She mentioned you this evening. Oh, don't worry, I'm not going to kill her. That was my intention, but it's far more satisfying to let her live." Fingers threaded through

Kate's hair, tracing the tender, healing skin there. "There will be other chances."

"Like me," Kate said.

Nails like claws digging into her scalp and tearing the scabs away, slicing at the skin over her sternum and ripping her blouse. "Yes."

"No." Kate tried to move. This time she really tried, her muscles tense in effort. But she could not move from where she stood before the mirror.

"You don't really want to leave," Mary whispered in her ear. She slid a hand under the torn fabric of her blouse and traced a line between Kate's breasts down to her navel. Her other hand began to deftly undo the buttons. Kate would be her fifth Chicago killing. Kate saw her own face on the news, some horrible, unremarkable photograph that no one would want to remember. "If you wanted to leave, you would be able to walk away without trouble. You could leave this room, this house. I only come when I'm called."

"I never called you," Kate said. Her voice sounded strange to her ears.

"Perhaps you don't remember. But I remember you. You weren't ready for me then. None of you were." Mary pulled Kate's sleeves down and dropped the blouse to the floor.

"Why are you … what happened to you?" She took in every cut on Mary's face and hands and every stain on her dress. "Did you do those yourself?"

Her skirt fell around her feet in a breath of fabric. Kate tried to cover herself, but her hands stayed listless at her side.

There was a slight hiss in her ear. "Of course I didn't do these to myself. But you will."

Mary unfastened her bra, and Kate was left standing in front of the mirror in just her panties.

"And this was what you were when I found you again, when you gave me your first taste," Mary said, resting her chin on

Kate's shoulder. Kate's hand moved of its own volition, cradling the weight of her stomach. The candlelight forgave some things, but not everything, and Kate was captivated. She saw the cuts all over Mary's face and her own good smooth skin. Mary caressed the length of her arm until her hand covered Kate's. She pushed Kate's hand down until her underwear joined the rest of the clothing on the floor. Mary's other hand grabbed hers and brought it to touch one flat breast.

"What are you doing?" Kate gasped.

"What you were never able to do," Mary said. "And what *he* certainly never did. Could you ever bring yourself to touch it?"

Kate felt her stomach lurch as Mary brought her hand further down, and there it was beneath her palm, moist, yielding, with its slight weight. Kate shut her eyes tight, and it made her sensation of touch more intense.

"See, that's not so bad," Mary murmured. "I cannot imagine what you were crying for when I came to you. What any of you cry for. You're what I look for. You're what I want."

Pressure in circles. And Mary let go of her hands.

With the first unbidden, unwanted surfacing of pleasure came the teeth into her breast, hard and sharp and keen. Had she screamed? Her eyes were open again, and her hand moved in circles, as though she were in a trance, lips parted, mouth glistening. Mary lifted her head and wiped the blood from her mouth with the back of her stained hand. She swallowed the piece of flesh in her mouth and looked into Kate's eyes through the reflection.

"Now," Mary said, "can you do the same for me?"

Kate reached back with her left hand but felt nothing but the wall.

"No," Mary said, and her laughter was clear, bright, and happy. Blue eyes glowed in the darkness. The invisible hand took hers again and brought it to the glass. "In the mirror."

Kate leaned against the counter, quivering and warm, pushed

against the mirror where she could see Mary's hand. She felt the skin: dry, substantial. Her head lowered as Mary kissed the back of her neck and brought the cold sharp edge of a blade against Kate's right thigh. *The kitchen knife I brought*, she thought distantly. Tension coiled delightfully, and fear made her intertwine her fingers with Mary's. Mary's face divided as the mirror cracked but merged again as Kate's blood shuddered onto her skin and into her mouth.

"Come into me," Mary whispered. She yanked the embedded blade up, and Kate thrust forward and shattered the mirror, falling through.

Your Stockholm Syndrome

Esther Mazakian

Zero to hero, her curves held too much meaning for you and
the damage not yet done. Militarily, force-
    feedings strip her
    of her last meal and you, your Sunday palms cool her feet,
     and she turns to
    you, the bitch at last

        in ankle shackles, in love, let's face it. Your bandages
and your stubble-sweat, so middle-eastern in a way, though
you're
from Arkansas.

         Perspiring and aspiring the dew on your hands
sets her livery saliva rivuletting

    through her
    between-breasts. Never had sex and food been so connected.

See her eyes stealing
    your one lazy leg like it was open prey; hungry

as you

       she says, Get the fuck down.

nascent fashion

Larissa Lai

it is dark and she
it is dark so thirsty and the smell
my own body their bodies all this rot
this shit this vomit this blood
i didn't know i wanted
wanted the white bed
was that so bad?
white bed all crisp cotton and down
high posts a girl
i could yell at
i'd make her pay make her
anger i didn't see
the mirror myself ghost
white bed for ghost girl
wanted to help my parents
wanted a girl to yell at
this girl this girl
it is dark and she
so thirsty the smell
hunger long gone
air cries crises gap
in the dark my body their bodies

old scarfaced bag that yells
at me i'll make her pay
the factory girl that pinches
the girl that cries that pricks her finger
that strains her eyes
the girl with chemical burns
the girl that suffocated the girl
the girl with the severed hand
the girl i want
not this dark
the white bed in the glossy
advertisement i saw and the white
girl in the white dress so pure
i wanted
not this ghost
a girl to do
what i say
not me

this sorrow in the innocent
part the longing
imperialism's imperative scathes
we dirt even in revolution
desire awry
we force we blood we maim
she body she collective
in our innocent we search
culture's purgative rhetoric
as machines repetitive wilt spirit
as bones dig mass racial graves
our soft that works tears burns
dismembered and bleeding
she dark she poor
this litany all tongue-stuck and word-full
innocent digs for itself
absolute abstract
calls to body's miraculous
pulse and warm this soft
reproduce kisses even the gentle
belly all blossom
pretend a fresh garden
sing the charred cell's
delectable mutation phantom
pleasure of severed limb
chant the cancer regenerative
our brilliant pustules recall brine
of origin the new salt
futures a city of soft
biological meteors replicate
scale our feather our alien
innocent all damp and downy

automaton dreams sightless lovers
maiden form from midden heap
cog gear apple dry leaf mildew
negative map of masculine longing
as tongues catch empty
eye sockets and severed hands
scamper free of corporate entities
i language my body to being
ontology's on-switch
tender as rubber nipple
my skin flushes
flesh full as any cyborg
i arm my machine love
swing from limbo to limbo
right up the river
my amazon lethal as yellow mud
breathe my golly
my salem sailor's
supernumerary tipple and
unheimlich familiar
witchy witchy woman
american as gene genie
i replicate my sweet helix
doubled and coiling
you've come a long way baby

demonic mnemonic
memory repeats
shell of abandoned girl
flushed fleshy to recall
the want not want shift
of this kiss that stirs
tumble into the crash
the break that can't
recollect pieces pulpy as
organisms indeterminate life
unsure of entry and sharp
as shrapnel
harmonic hysteric mystic as
eleusis lucidly remembers
future descent into death
forgetful father's rail of corpses
open wounds protruding bones
that litter occupied streets
bedrooms of houses turned in by children
shattered girls left in stairwells
our good attempts to patch to hide
under a fine layer of leaves
forget to tell the girl
kisses are the plumb line to horror
the first word is silent soft
this gentle call to loss
we girls who understand
dress as boys our armour
hard thick our tongues that cut
raw inside layered under
repeats insistent litany
desire as tomorrow's memory
ghosting visits our soft mouths wait for

Sido

Suki Lee

I heard that French women are easy, and I think I just found one. A skin-tight T-shirt and jeans hug the nymphlike curves of her body. A short pixie cut frames her staggeringly beautiful face. She's completely sexed and looks about thirty. Best of all, she's leaning in the open apartment door, looking me up and down like I'm a piece of meat.

"*Bonjour*," the sylph says.

"I don't speak French," I shrug apologetically, putting my bags down.

I'm winded from walking seven flights up the long spiral wooden staircase to the landing. From there, I had to go through a door and up a ladder to the apartment. Perched on top of an old eighteenth-century building, it's a bit of an odd place, somewhat resembling a birdhouse.

"Sido Lebris?" I inquire. I'm expecting someone much older than the nubile woman standing before me.

"Yes, zat's me of course." She turns on her heels and leads me with a swaying walk into the apartment.

The open loft has two massive barred windows that overlook the city's silver rooftops. Upstairs is an attic crawl space that will serve as my bedroom during my week-long stay in Paris.

"I guess you're wanting your rent." I pull out the money. I

can't help staring at my new landlady. Her sexy body makes me feel crazily alive.

She takes the cash, and looks directly at me. "You want to fuck me? Is zat what you want?" I'm amazed by her directness. I pass her the euros, and watch her erect nipples under her T-shirt. Looking at me with a flirtatious gaze, I get a jolt when she adds, "I bet you taste good."

Sido walks up to me so we're almost touching. I'm electrified. She takes the back of my head and brings my mouth to hers, giving me a rough, raunchy kiss. I'm completely overwhelmed by the inside of her mouth. Its hot, wet velvet sets me off. Then suddenly she bites down on the inside of my lip.

"That hurt," I protest.

Sido steps back, regarding me with amusement. Her tits are so hot that I feel sick to my stomach. "Here are zee keys." She drops them in my palm, and leaves.

I'm lying on an uncomfortable bed, which is no more than four feet from the skylight. The window is full of scratches. Feathers have lodged inside the wooden frame. When caught in the wind, they whirl around like small satellite dishes sending signals. My lip is swollen where Sido bit it. My mind keeps reiterating our kiss—the absolute eroticism of her wet mouth and her unswerving directness. I wonder if this is how she treats all her tenants. I masturbate and think about her while looking out at the dramatic clouds over the city. She's the sexiest woman I've ever seen.

I sleep off the jetlag for hours. It's dusk when I'm awakened by the creaking of the wooden ladder up to the loft. I listen to the groaning of the rungs until the presence of someone in my room is palpable. I open my eyes and gather the blankets around me.

"What are you doing here?"

"I thought you would have left by now," my nefarious landlady explains calmly, while scrutinizing me in bed.

"You can't just come here," I protest. "I rented the apartment for the week."

"I need to feed zee *chouettes*," Sido states, matter-of-factly.

"I don't speak French," I remind her.

"Owls. Zey come every night, because I feed zem."

"You feed them?"

"I leave zem something to eat outside zee window," Sido says, gesturing at the skylight.

"Something? Like what?"

"Mice, from my apartment." Sido gestures with the plastic bag in her hand, which contains a few of their still, tiny bodies.

"You shouldn't do that. Owls are wild animals."

"Zey are majestic and beautiful creatures—and my friends."

Sido has the edge of a tear in her eye, which makes her all the more sexy. It confirms not only that I'm attracted to her, but also that she's somewhat unhinged.

"Anyways, I think it's wrong for you to come here," I tell her.

"Are you sure? You don't want to fuck me?" Sido asks, looking at me with her sultry brown eyes. I hesitate, and within that moment, she puts the plastic bag down and descends the ladder. "Put zee mice outside zee window for zee owls tonight!" she calls up to me from the floor below. Then she is gone.

I get out of bed and throw out the disgusting plastic bag. I also organize my suitcase, so I'll know if Sido's been through it when I get back. I'm determined not to get involved with her. She's trouble.

It's early evening by the time I venture out into the beauty of Paris. I wander past ornate buildings and statues encumbered by roosting birds. Couples kissing voraciously on the city's curvy medieval streets get me ruminating about my seductive landlady. Despite Sido's oddness, I'm brooding over her pornographic body and her sense of entitlement. I crave her like a sinful meal.

Night is falling, so I decide to go to Troisième Lieu for distraction. It's a women's bar I read about. When I arrive, it doesn't disappoint. The long narrow space is packed with women in conversation, eating, drinking, dancing, and kissing. I take a place at the bar and order an absinthe from the hot bartender. My gaze flits from one woman to the next, and I drink up the sight of all the lithe French bodies in this oasis. Eventually, part of me realizes that I'm searching for that hustler, Sido, amidst all this beauty. I feel uneasy that she's entered my subconscious, so I flirt with the bartender, who flirts back. Eventually, a few women draw me into their conversation.

"I don't speak French," I explain.

They switch to English and ask questions about my stay.

While they're inquiring about my apartment, I interject, "Are there owls in Paris?"

"Owls in Paris? Never. Zey live far from here, in zee country," says Sylvie, a lecherous older woman who's already whispered that she wants to take me home tonight.

"My landlady claims that she keeps owls in the city," I explain.

"Impossible! Zis person is making up stories," slurs drunken Véronique, who is androgynously attractive.

Later in the evening, Véronique corners me. She points to her right cheek and says, "Give me a kiss here." I do.

She points to her left cheek. "Give me a kiss here."

She points to her lips. "Now give me a kiss here."

We kiss for a long time.

But in the end, it doesn't end up amounting to anything. My kiss with Véronique is disappointing and makes me hunger for Sido's mouth. I'm exhausted and the jetlag is catching up with me, so I decide to leave. I walk alone past crowds of people carousing in the chaotic Parisian streets. Close to my apartment, I see two men working furiously to undo each other's pants in a doorway. It seems that the entire city is sexed.

When I get back to the apartment, it is quiet. I check my belongings. Everything is as I left it. I go to bed, relieved that Sido didn't intrude. All the same, the shadow of her kiss is still with me. I fantasize about eating her out while she's naked and standing against the kitchen counter in high heels.

I'm almost asleep when I hear a haunting call in the night: a long-drawn-out *hooo*, an uncomfortable silence, and then a startling *ha!* The sounds ricochet off the walls of my room, and make me shudder. There's a flapping sound outside the window, and I open my eyes just as the beast's wingspan blocks the moon and it comes to rest on the roof. The owl is perched on the edge of the skylight. Two massive furrowed brows come together over a hooked beak. A circular facial disk of feathers frames huge, dark eyes. A puffed-up chest rises above me. For a moment, I consider putting the mice out, but then the owl scratches at the window with a clawed foot, which I find unnerving. I'm about to move to the downstairs couch when the bird spreads its wings and lifts itself into the Parisian sky. It's hours before I'm able to sleep.

It's noon and harsh daylight is funnelling through the skylight. I step cautiously down the ladder to the bathroom. The shower is a small confined space. I relax in the steaming hot water and plan my day ahead—an omelette at a café, an exhibition at Musée d'Orsay, a walk along the Seine, and maybe dinner at Troisième Lieu.

My thoughts are interrupted when Sido opens the door and comes into the bathroom completely naked. Her clothes are in her arms, and she puts them down at her feet.

"What are you doing!? You can't just come in here!" I shout.

I try not to look at the curve of her hips, her chiselled collarbone, her lean arms, the muscle and bone of her sex.

"You didn't feed zee owls!" she accuses me loudly over the sound of the shower.

Sido looks like a mirage through the dense steam. My body responds to her against my will. The more I look at her, the wetter I get.

"You have to leave." I turn off the shower.

"Turn zee water back on!" she orders firmly.

"No. You have to leave." She's making me angry. I feel humiliated standing there naked and exposed. I open the narrow shower doors. "Leave now or I'm calling the police."

Sido's eyes light up with fury, which turns me on despite my better judgment. She reaches into her pile of clothes on the floor and pulls out a gun. Holding it with two hands, she points it at my gut. I recoil and back against the shower. "You didn't feed zee owls. So now zee water goes back on, and you turn around." Sido is flushing with anger.

I do as she says. Hot water streams down my shoulder as I face the wall with my back to her. My heart flips.

"Spread your legs," Sido commands.

I obey. The space between us closes as she steps into the shower with me. She pushes the gun against my ass. I'm shaking as I wait for the explosion. It doesn't come. Instead, she kneels below me. I think about kicking her, but am suddenly jolted when her hand searches between my legs. She pulls me open and plunges her fingers inside me. I brace myself against the wall as she forces herself into my cunt, pumping back and forth, each movement a burst of pain. All the same, I'm wet and I can't help moving with her. Sido puts even more of her hand inside me, and my body takes her in. She fucks me with cruelty, plowing into me with everything she's got. I'm helplessly driven to pleasure and ejaculate standing up. My cunt pulses and my come flows over Sido's hand as she holds it inside me. She releases me, then stands up and turns off the shower.

She puts her arms around me. "*Mon amour*," my brutish landlady purrs. She gently cradles one of my breasts with one hand while the other holds the weapon against my chest. I look down and see that it's a child's toy gun.

Of course, I realize that my landlady has just raped me, but the feeling of her skin against mine sent me into orbit. To my surprise, I find it difficult to kick Sido out of the apartment after that. Her beauty makes her sick mind worth tolerating.

It's a sweltering day in Paris. Thirsty birds tip their heads back in silence on the streets. Walking is painful and sitting even more so. My cunt is a raw, pulverized piece of meat, yet I can't stop thinking about her. She seems to have eclipsed everything else. I'm obsessed and unmotivated to explore the city, so I guiltily skulk into the darkness of Troisième Lieu.

Not many people are in the bar in the early afternoon. I make eye contact with the bartender and slump at the bar to flirt with her. "You should come home with me," she suggests charmingly.

"Maybe another time," I decline, even though it would be a thrill to have her fuck me.

"Are you sure?" The sexy server is clearly never declined.

I nod.

"You have someone?" she asks.

"I have something." Since she's probably heard it all, I decide to tell her about being held up by Sido with the toy gun in the shower.

"It was just a game," she pronounces.

"She manipulated me."

"You like zat, maybe."

She's right of course. I can't escape the grip that Sido has on me. My pull to her is fierce, even though she acts like she despises me. After several more drinks, I leave the bar late without really having noticed that it became filled with beautiful women.

Back at the apartment, I lie under the skylight, and wait for Sido's pet. Tonight, there are two owls. They are aggressive and repeatedly bellow *coo-wik!* while scratching at the window. This time, I look back at them. It makes me feel like I'm under Sido's cruel gaze, and it turns me on.

"Where were you last night?" Sido's arms are crossed, her jaw is clenched, her eyes are on fire.

I blink at her from the bed. She looks quite out of her mind, and yells at me in French. The language sounds beautiful in her mouth, and I find her fiery rage exciting. Nevertheless, I interrupt. "What are you talking about?"

She looks at me with disgust. "I left a note and some mice for you to feed zee owls, and you didn't—again!"

I am weighing the situation. Sido is wearing a tight camisole that shows off the sexy curve of her shoulders. Her mouth, reddened by lipstick, has the most luscious curves. I could easily kiss her—or kick her out.

"Let me punish you," she says, with a wild look in her eyes.

The thought of her libidinous body next to mine excites me. Something in me responds to being humiliated by her. Perhaps it's that I want to be corrupted by whatever it is that has corrupted her. Sido kneels down to me. Her face is stone cold. I want her on the bed with her ass in the air. I want to fuck her from behind and make her scream. In the middle of my fantasy, she takes off her camisole, revealing her torso, which is chiselled like a Greek statue. She's cut like a piece of meat. Her breasts look buoyant.

"Do you want to be punished?"

Sido pulls off her skirt, revealing her voluptuous ass crack, which is accentuated by a floss of G-string. I feel a sick attraction to the violent subtext of her gaze.

"Yes, punish me."

"Lie on your back and spread your arms out," she orders.

"You first." I move to kiss her.

She raises her hand, and slaps me viciously across my face and eyes. I'm in shock, and fall backwards on the bed, in harrowing pain. I want to see how bad it is, how much damage she's done. Disoriented, I try to get up so I can get away from Sido, but she swoops down and straddles me. She's stronger than I would have guessed and forces her weight on me until I'm lying back on the bed. I try to fight her, but my face feels like it's bleeding.

I'm bucking her off me when, in the midst of the struggle, Sido's body language suddenly shifts, and she thrusts her wet cunt on my naked abdomen, making a mewing sound of titillation. We stop fighting each other. She leans over my mouth and kisses me deeply. My body responds with limp submission, and I stretch my arms out on either side of me.

"Zat's better," Sido coos in my ear.

She binds my wrists to the legs of the bed with rope, then reaches into the bedside table and pulls out a harness and strap-on. I am splayed out before her like an offering. Sido kisses every part of my body except my mouth. Wordlessly, she places the harness on me and pulls the straps taut, fastening the buckles around my legs. As she adjusts the apparatus, the cock rises erect on my pubis into a massive hard-on.

"Your punishment is not to move," Sido commands, as she very tenderly touches my face where she struck me. "You understand?"

"Yes," I gasp, my skin aching beneath her touch.

With her legs spread on either side of me, Sido walks herself over the cock and teases her cunt over it. She leans back against my knees, so I have a perfect view of the pink areolas of her luscious tits. I feel primitive when the tip disappears into her, but I don't move. Breathing heavily with excitement, Sido takes in more of the cock, and with one strong thrust of her hips, slips its entire length into her. The bewitching look of pleasure on her face makes me want to come. She rides me, bucking up and down, plunging me into her pussy. The base of the harness pushes against me. My clit is hard and inflamed. I don't move even though I want to fuck her hard. When Sido comes, she throws her head back and howls in a low guttural noise that doesn't sound human. I come during her long orgasm, but I don't move or make a sound. Sido collapses next to me all, sweaty and spent. Her exquisite body thrusts post-coitally against my hip for several minutes.

After a moment, Sido undoes the rope. Making little cooing noises, she kisses my wrists, running her tongue along them. At one point, she looks into my eyes, lingering on the one that she struck.

"Will you hit me?" she asks in her sexiest voice.

"Hit you?"

"I want to be punished for what I did to you." She starts tearing up.

I stroke her short hair and the beautiful sloping nape of her neck.

"I love you," she tells me tearfully, and spreads her legs. We writhe around the geography of the bed. At the end of it, I get between her legs and make her come over and over again. Her labia are like two beautiful outspread wings, and I can't get enough. We hold each other tightly as we fall asleep, but I wake up alone.

In the afternoon, a few hours later, I'm dizzy when I open my eyes. My face is all swollen around my eye and mouth. I keep coaxing myself to get out of bed, but it hurts to move. I finally make it to the bathroom and look in the mirror. I don't recognize the person looking back. My eyelid is bulging, making me look ogreish. My lips are swollen and it hurts to wince.

I agonize over what to do, but every time I look in the mirror at my puffed-up face, the answer is clear. I have to go to the police and file a complaint against Sido. The ferocity with which she hit me was totally out of control.

At a station in the neighbourhood, I wait for a long time with dozens of people before my number flashes up on the screen. When I get to the front desk, the officer gazes impassively at my bruised face. "I'd like to report an incident," I tell him. "I was assaulted."

"Luc?" he calls over to the officer beside him. "*Quelqu'un qui parle anglais.*"

The officer who speaks English summons me over and checks out my eye with the same indifference. He takes notes as I tell him about Sido assaulting me, but I leave out the sex part.

After a while he stops writing and looks up at me. "Why not tell her to leave?"

"I have."

"Lock zee door."

"She has a key."

"We'll look into it," he sighs. "It could take a while. You might want to leave in zee meantime. Stay in a hotel."

I knew he was going to tell me to leave—it's the advice any rational person should take. Despite the rational part of my mind, the irrational side wants to stay in the apartment and fuck Sido.

I take a long, slow walk back to the apartment. It's a sunny day, and I'm feeling optimistic. I stop at a café for a sandwich and a glass of wine. After I'm done, I decide to pick up my laptop so I can check my email and catch up on a few things.

The second I get back, I notice that something's not right. My coat isn't hanging from the hook, my computer isn't at the kitchen table, almost all my toiletries have been taken, and the fridge has been emptied of food. I rush up the ladder to check for my passport, and discover that the loft has been emptied. All of my luggage is gone.

There's a note from Sido on my bed. "You didn't feed the owls, so now I punish you. And you were stupid to go to the police."

A sick part of me loves that she followed my movements through the city. I want to see how far she'll go. Just then, the front door clicks shut, and I hear it being locked from the outside.

I am in a prison from which there is no escape—there is no phone and the windows are all barred. I spend the rest of that day shouting for help. The apartment is perched on top of the building, so none of the tenants below hear me. Eventually, I go hoarse, and my plea turns to a low, raspy whisper.

The second day, I come up with a different plan. I break one of the large barred windows and yell as loudly as I can to the street below. This time my voice is carried up into the sky as soon as it leaves my mouth. I am quite alone with the shattered glass and the cool Parisian wind surging through the sharp, jagged hole.

By the third day, I realize that Sido has no intention of releasing me. I wash my clothes in the sink and lay them out to dry. Even though it's midday, I go to sleep. There's nothing else to do. Except eat.

Sido leaves me delicious meals by the front door every day. Mostly it's fattening food such as large, undercooked pieces of red meat, baguettes and Camembert, and chocolate croissants from the bakery. She also leaves me several bottles of wine, which I always polish off effortlessly. I gain weight.

The days blend together as I lose track of time. It's always the same. I wake in the morning and walk around the apartment for hours until I'm exhausted and the room starts spinning. The rest of the day is spent reading out loud—books by Collette, Victor Hugo, and Albert Camus. They're all in French, and I don't understand a word, but I read them phonetically to pass the time. The sound of my voice struggling with French pronunciation is comforting, and quells my growing desire to talk to myself. As soon as the sun sets, I go to sleep. The owls staring at me through the skylight are the only creatures keeping me company. I've grown accustomed to their voracious gaze and their still, patient presence.

Sido and I don't cross paths, and I never hear her leave my meals. I realize that she must have a way of monitoring me, because she leaves food only while I'm asleep. I turn the apartment upside down and find two hidden cameras, one in the kitchen and one in the loft.

Those cameras are my only way of communicating with her. I do my best with the *français-anglais* dictionary, and write single stark words on pieces of paper that I hold up to the camera for hours on end. *Arrêter. Aider. Libérer. S'il vous plaît.* Finally, I write, "*Voulez-vous coucher avec moi?*" and it works.

One evening I wake after a long nap to find Sido in the kitchen. She's sitting at the table, which is set with a large meal. I take a seat opposite her without protesting. She's got a handgun, and this time it's real.

Sido raises her glass in a toast. "*Santé,*" she says, looking deeply into my eyes. I look back into her insane gaze and am shocked that I still find her so incredibly attractive.

"Why did you go to zee police?" Sido asks in gentle tones. "You should not have done zat," she admonishes me tenderly. She takes a sip of wine, while keeping the handgun pointed at me. "Zere's no need to be afraid. If you're not enjoying zis, zen we go our separate ways. It's simple."

We eat in silence. She unhurriedly nibbles at her meal, while I devour mine. It's three days since she brought food, and I'm starving.

"So?" she asks, after I'm finished eating.

"So?" I look at the gun.

"Would you like dessert?" Sido reaches over and squeezes my arm with the hand that's not holding the gun.

"Like what?"

"Like me," she suggests seductively.

I feel shaky. I don't need to have sex with Sido, I need to escape from her. At the same time, I'd be a liar if I didn't admit that the idea of fucking her at gunpoint arouses me.

"Is zat a yes, or am I going to have to shoot you?" Sido aims the gun at my head.

"It's a yes."

Sido gestures for me to stand and tells me to go to the bathroom to get my electric toothbrush. She also directs me to bring a bottle of wine and the wine glass beside it. With my hands full, I can't defend myself. I do as she bids and climb slowly up into the loft. Sido follows behind.

"Pour us some wine," she instructs once we're up there. She presses the barrel of the gun to my heart, and extends the glass she brought with her.

I fill her glass, then my own, and sit on the edge of the bed. She holds me at gunpoint while I drink.

"Take your clothes off, lie on zee bed, and open your legs," Sido commands.

I do as she says. She kneels between my legs. Not for one second does she take the gun off me.

"Follow all my orders or I'll shoot you," she warns. "Understand?"

"I understand," I say, but I'm getting wet with Sido between my legs. She positions the handgun inside my cunt. My body just lets it slide in. Then she takes my electric toothbrush and turns it on. She holds the back of it to my clit. It vibrates against me and feels like a huge revving motor. It gets me to a place of stimulation without foreplay, without any tenderness whatsoever. A large orgasm explodes out of me.

After a while, Sido withdraws the gun from my cunt and looks at me expectantly.

I'm feeling like I might fall asleep any second.

"I knew you'd like dessert," Sido says to me, smiling and pointing the handgun at her own head.

I struggle to focus on her. Everything is becoming fuzzy and my eyes are closing. I'm fighting hard, but I know it's a battle I'm going to lose. She doctored my wine.

I can't move. There's a gag in my mouth. Sido has tied me to the bed, using rope to fasten my wrists and legs to it.

The skylight is wide open, so I'm exposed to the outdoors. High above is the dark Parisian night and the moon shining down upon me. Two owls are circling, their wailing, sinister cries getting closer. *Ha!* they repeat over and over again.

I can vaguely make out that a blanket is covering me. My vision momentarily comes into focus, and I see that it's not a blanket. I'm covered by dead mice. Sido is sitting by my side, taking one dead mouse carcass after another out of plastic bags, and laying their cold little cadavers on my naked body.

When I look at her, part of me still wants her. She's so beautiful.

Crabby

Michelle Tea

When Steph and I came back to Boston that summer, we started working for Madame Lynne again, and we moved into a one-room apartment in Provincetown, at the edge of Cape Cod. You couldn't really call it an apartment; it was just a single room.

I had crabs in my crotch. Pubic lice, down in my hair there. They didn't really itch. I was sitting on the toilet in the communal bathroom on the second floor that I had to share with everyone else in the house—the straight kids who drank and worked too much, the conservative gay guy with the even tan, the bleach-blonde dyke who worked at the leather store, and the quiet girl on the first floor with the boyfriend who stalked her. He often came to our house after the bars let out and banged on her door with the cast his broken arm was wrapped up in until one of the boys woke up and went down to talk to him down. And he would start crying really loud, just blubbering, half-yelling stuff, and somebody else would wake up and go across the street to the pay phone in the parking lot and finally call the cops. This happened all the time. The cops would gently escort him out of our house. Steph and I just listened to the whole thing from our futon and grumbled, "Jesus Christ." We talked a little about how much we hated men, then went back to sleep.

But the bathroom, it was actually pretty clean considering

how many people used it. I was sitting there peeing when I saw *it* and I thought it was just a fleck of nature, like a bit of seaweed from being in the ocean, or sand. And I looked at it and I picked at it. It seemed to stick to me, and I noticed it had legs, tiny ones poking out from its side like a crab. I made a swift connection between my pubic hair and this thing that actually really looked like a little fucking crab, and I screamed, "Steph!" She was upstairs hitting the bong. She said she knew right when she heard me scream like that, that I had crabs. She came *thump thump thump* down the stairs then *rattle rattle* at the bathroom door. I hopped off the toilet and waddled over with my underwear looped around my knees and pee dripping down my thighs, I unlatched the door and it felt like the dirtiest moment in the world. I started crying like crazy, greeting Steph there at the threshold of my nightmare, dripping from my face and crotch. I gulped, "I think I have crabs."

She said, "Get in there," and pushed me back into the little bathroom—the temple of hygiene with its many faucets and soaps and foaming bottles. Steph locked the door and I plopped back on the bowl.

I hadn't really had many moral twinges about me and Steph's prostitution, none of the failing self-esteem and self-worth that were supposed to accompany a girl into such a profession. It was too easy. I would look into the mirror and think, *I am a prostitute*, and wait for an appropriate wave of horror and revulsion. I would wait and wait and feel nothing.

But this was like all the pangs of guilt and conscience I never had took the form of parasitic bugs and burst forth from my crotch. *That's what you get*, I thought. Steph crouched by the bowl and poked around at me, pinching a small monster out with her fingertips. "Yup, you have crabs."

"Steph," I sobbed. "They really look just like little crabs!"

She hiked up her hippie dress and brought her pantiless crotch over to my face. "Do you see anything, do you see anything?" I searched through her hair like my mother checking my head for nits in kindergarten. I remember she had a certain comb for it, white plastic, and how poisonous the shampoo smelled—it was called Kwell, a word that sounds like a bug. The whole neighbourhood and extended family had gathered in my kitchen for the big soap, my head bent into the sink, suffocating beneath the shampoo fumes and water. My grandparents were there; it was a real big deal. Afterward, all the adults sat around drinking tea and chain-smoking, speculating on which filthy child could have passed me the bugs. "They jump," my grandmother kept saying. I imagined them with small and powerful legs, big as the magnified picture that came with the shampoo instructions.

"Soap and water don't cost nothing," my mother clucked, disgust in her voice.

"Soap costs," I protested, sticking my long wet hair into my nose, breathing the awful stink of it.

"Anyone can afford soap," my mother insisted. "It doesn't cost anything to be clean." They went on about who let their kids run around wild and how Chelsea was going to hell.

It was all about dirt in this really moral, really virtuous way, and it was what I sat with, trapped in the bathroom in Provincetown as Steph ran down to Adam's Pharmacy to buy razors.

What else did I know about lice, about crabs? They were evidence of betrayal.

After my parents divorced, but before my father disappeared—just before I hit my teen years—we were attempting to have a very 1980s divorced family, a visit-dad-on-the-weekends situation, but Dad was such a jerk—a couple cans of Miller from the fridge, and he'd start trying to pry information out of us: Who was our mother's boyfriend, did he sleep over, did he buy her the car he'd seen her driving—a powder-blue Escort with a hatchback—and who said I could go to Chelsea High and not Pope John or Saint Rose, why wasn't that discussed with him? He was my father. Did I discuss it with my mother's boyfriend? And my breathing got all funny and I noticed the faster I breathed the funnier I felt in my head, and it was like when I forgot to eat in the summer and then went out riding my bike until I saw spots in front of my eyes and fell over. I figured if I kept breathing faster and funnier I'd pass out and my dad would have to leave me alone. "Jesus Christ," he sounded annoyed. Through my fuzzy eyes I could see my sister looking panicked, and I wished she would get it and faint with me so we could go home, and Dad would be the big asshole for bothering his daughters until they were sick with it. I feigned unconsciousness for a few minutes. I was sprawled on that weird piece of furniture, Dad's first bachelor pad acquisition, sort of a couch but long like a bed and covered in long orange fake fur. It looked a bit like a sports car. I came to, and he called us a cab.

Madeline, my sister, was so upset and excited, she burst into our house shouting, "Michelle passed out!" Breathlessly she explained it all to Ma while I stood there and tried to look dizzy.

Ma got right on the phone to Dad, and they had a huge fight. I slipped into my bedroom and quietly lifted my powder-blue telephone—same colour as the new Escort. I placed the phone to my ear and heard him call her a douche bag. "Don't you talk to her like that!" I yelled at him.

"Michelle, get off the phone!" they both hollered at me. And Ma was crying. Things rose into hysteria quickly at my house, a manic, buoyant heat. My mother was crying, which meant I couldn't. We couldn't all be crying. She hung up the phone, the beige one that hung on the wall in the kitchen.

She went into the bathroom and sat there on the toilet, leaving the door open. Her white nurse's uniform was hiked up her thighs, a wad of toilet paper waiting in her hand. She blotted her teary face with it. "Are you okay?" she asked. I nodded. "You're not going to faint again?" She seemed nervous about it. I couldn't tell if I'd faked it or if it had been real.

"I'm okay," I said. I wanted her to shut the bathroom door, so

I could steal one of her cigarettes and smoke it.

"I don't want to turn you against your father," she said, which meant she was about to tell me something good. "I'll tell you everything that happened when you're older. I don't want to talk badly about him, he's still your father," she stalled.

"Ma, it's okay, I don't even like him." It was true. Dad was rapidly becoming the biggest jerk in the world. It was hard to forgive him for kicking us all out of our house, hard to visit him and see the room that used to be mine, empty now but for a few cardboard boxes—a half-assed storage space. In his new living room I'd watched MTV on the colour television, but we were watching a miniscule black-and-white job back at our new place. A small screen of static. Dad had cable. There was Mick Jagger, walking his weird turkey-walk through some inner-city neighbourhood. "I ain't waiting on a lady," he sang. "I'm just waiting on a friend."

"That's my song," Dad said bitterly, his words coming out on a cloud of exhaled Vantage. "Not waiting for a lady."

He scared me then, the contempt in his voice when he said "lady," the lift of the beer can to his wide, Polish mouth. Now, looking back, I'm struck by his ability to be moved by a rock song, that he was listening hard enough to hear the lyrics through the nasal British accent, that he related. The song comforted him in his evil, alcoholic mood. He was standing behind the bar he'd bought when Ma convinced him that we should at least have the living room furniture. We got the scratchy floral couch and the rickety armchair. He replaced it with a bar and the weird fluffy sofa-bed-thing. On the bar sat a box of Andes mints, the only food in the house. Later we'd go out for a bucket of Kentucky Fried Chicken and eat it on the floor in front of the television. For now I sucked on the cool, minty chocolates. It was the last time we visited Dad.

"When you kids were little he gave me crabs," Ma finally said. "He said that I gave them to him." Ma was really crying now, wiping at her cheeks with the toilet paper. "I was always faith-ful to him," she said, and I believed her. She gulped and sobbed. Probably she never got to really cry about it. "Don't you ever spread your legs for anybody!" she yelled. Not angrily, just to get her point across. I nodded and slipped a cigarette slyly from her pack.

Steph came back to the bathroom with a little paper bag. It had plastic razors in it—pink for girls—and also a can of girl-scented shaving cream, a pearly-pink gel that lathered into a soapy paste. "Oh God!" I cried more, looking at the stuff. I just wanted something to come and make the crabs be gone. Make them never have been there.

"I'm going to shave too," Steph said. Steph was such a martyr. There weren't any bugs in her crotch. I could never have a trag-edy of my own; she was always trying to one-up me. "I could have eggs," she insisted. We tried to remember if we'd seen any of the same tricks. We slept in the same bed, but we never had sex anymore. I was sure she didn't have the crabs.

We crowded naked into the shower, which was like an alu-minum closet. There was barely room for us both. To get at the tricky places we had to stretch our legs out onto the bathroom floor, getting the whole place wet. Steph was scared of the razor, but I understood you couldn't just lop your clit off the way she feared. I brought the razor down over my pubic bone, instantly clogging it with thick curls I then had to dig from the metal and fling into the drain. I hated Steph for blubbering. You really couldn't have something shitty happen to you without her steal-ing all the glory. I just wanted to die thinking about those gross things latched onto my skin with their little teeth, drinking my blood.

"I quit," I said to Steph. "I'm not going to whore anymore."

"I'm not quitting," Steph snapped, getting all tough on me. She plunged the razor bravely into her wet hair. "They're just bugs." It would all be another battle scar for Steph, one more way for her to lord it over the rest of the world who would never know hardship the way she had known hardship. She tossed a soggy mat of hair to the floor and squirted more shaving gel into her palm. She bent down to inspect my work. "You got to get all of it," she said, pointing to the stubble. "That's where the eggs are." I lathered up and scraped some more. My skin was raw beneath the metal. "No, you really got to get rid of it," she said when my razor brought away nothing.

"Can't we just get some Kwell?" I pleaded. I was starting to whimper.

"Do you know how toxic that is!" Steph snapped. "That shit's poison, it's insecticide! Here," she took her razor, dug it into my skin. "You have to shave it clean." Little beads of blood formed on my pores. "Lift your leg." She ducked beneath me to get in the folds of my labia. I spread my butt cheeks, and angled the thing around my anus. It was like she was shaving the skin away.

"Steph! You can't," I cried. "It just hurts too much."

"If we don't get it now we'll have to do it all over again," she said simply. Steph was a Virgo. "Do me," she said once my entire genital area was shorn and burning. It looked like a hunk of chicken lying in the meat case. When we were through we took toilet paper and wiped up the mounds of hair that clogged the drain, the tiny drowning crabs. The paper melted in my hand as I flung the awful mess into the toilet.

Upstairs in our small, airless room we tried to find clothes that hadn't been worn since our last laundry. I had a yellow skirt, long and flowing, that crepey, hippie material. Everything else got stuffed into trash bags. We stripped the futon. There were no laundromats in Provincetown at the time, something about the water level or the ecosystem. Normally we brought our laundry into Boston and washed it in the laundry room in the brothel, but Steph wasn't due to work again for another week, and I had quit. "You're not really going to quit," Steph said cynically, like I was talking about smoking.

We brought our trash bags of contaminated laundry over to the wash-n-fold to be shipped out and returned clean in three days. "Make sure to use hot water," Steph said to the lady, and she smiled a queasy little smile at us.

Of course, Steph turned the whole infestation into a giant excuse to go shopping. We needed underwear, silk underwear that would feel nice against our burning cooches. We walked into the expensive lingerie store on Commercial Street with the sales ladies who always looked like they wanted to kick us out. Every time I took a step my crotch stung like a hive of bees. Steph dropped a hundred bucks on a bunch of drawers. "We deserve it," she said. A soft pile of panties sat on the counter, all different colours, the coolest, most tender material. Next Steph needed coconut oil, a dense jar of it, to smear on her traumatized labia. Then we needed to have an expensive dinner at the pricey Italian restaurant, way down where Commercial Street got quiet and pretty. We ate homemade sorbet—lemon and orange—served in the hollowed-out skins of the appropriate fruit.

That night we laid on our futon beneath a single clean sheet. Steph slid her hands beneath her new silk underwear and smeared her cunt with coconut oil. I did the same. It did make it feel better. "I'm going to masturbate," Steph announced.

It seemed strange to just lie there uninvolved while this was happening, so I said, "Me too," and rubbed the fragrant oil around my clit.

"You don't have to," Steph said, annoyed. She always thought I was jumping her train.

In the morning we lay naked at the beach, in a tiny forest of sea grass. Every time a sand flea hopped on my body I jumped. Steph had picked up a magnifying glass at the drugstore. She held it up to my irritated pussy and found an egg, a single fucking egg, like the tiniest glass bubble, stuck to a piece of stubble up by my butt hole. "No!" I wailed, and burst into tears again. Some fags passed by and looked at us curiously.

"We have to get rid of it," she said.

"I can't go through that again! I want Kwell."

At the pay phone in the parking lot across from our building we dialled the ASK-A-NURSE hotline. The nurse said we needed Kwell. "What if we shaved the area?" Steph suggested.

The nurse said, "No, no, you need to shampoo."

"You're just a pawn of western medicine!" Steph slammed the phone.

"The active ingredient in Kwell is flower extract," I suggested hopefully.

The other tenants at our place looked embarrassed when they saw us in the hallway. Certainly they knew we had crabs. Steph lathered up my ass again and raked the raw skin, and it was the worst feeling you could imagine. "There can't be anything left," I cried. Would Steph torture me? Was she that evil? She took the magnifying glass and inspected me deeply and promised that this time I was okay. We threw away the newly contaminated underwear and bought another pile. We went out to dinner at a seafood shack and ordered up a bunch of crab.

in your arms forever

Courtney Trouble

i work in the comfort of my delicate lace slip, a half-buttoned secretary's blouse, sheer panties, and classic black heels. my lips are slightly stained and glossy, and my eyes are dark and heavy. i know you would appreciate these details if you were still alive. you would have savoured them slowly as though they were your last fix. and I would indulge you, as always.

i haven't touched your flesh in forever, but my fingertips know your shape by heart. when i let loose another button, my fingers brush my nipple and it hardens immediately. i am wondering what your nipples feel like right now, safe inside your threadbare sunday dress, safe in your box under the ground. probably quite stiff.

oh, how i wish i were there with you, watching you sleep. your face would reveal your ancestry; the softest and whitest, with flushed cheeks, still, and tiny maps of veins decorating your empty body. your lips would still taste like delicious rose essence, and even in this stiff office chair i can feel myself melting underneath them. your doll eyes are as clear as a seer's crystal ball and twice as deceiving. the thought of you so far away from me starves my brain, and i find myself lighting yet another cigarette. you are to blame for all of my current addictions, and i have no intention of letting go.

another button gone, and in my mind you appear beneath me, wearing nothing but back-seam stockings tugging gently on a garter belt and a black vintage bra taut around your ribs. you look classic, in black and white, a darling vintage pinup with blonde hair falling in your face and a look in your eyes that would kill a weaker woman.

with all the powers of my lucid dream, you are suddenly real. my left heel is dangling off my toes while you trace my foot. the shock of your hands on my skin at long last sends a sudden alarm to my crotch. your eyes wander up my touch-hungry legs, searching for the source of my new awareness. i realize how badly i need you as i suck harder and harder on my skinny cigarette. my entire body is responding to the thrill of my fantasy; your ghost has given me goose bumps.

you rest your head in my lap for a moment before placing kisses all down my thighs and calves, down to the painted red tips of my toes. bring one into your mouth, send those tender sexual shivers back up my legs, look up at me with those crystal eyes. i want you to follow my shivers with your tongue, follow the scent of your prey.

i spread my legs and slide my ass down to the very edge of my office chair. your nose is pressed up against the crotch of my panties and you let out a whimper. you need it, you're begging for it with your fucking perfect eyes, and i can't help but tease you a second longer. a giggle and a puff of smoke later and you are whispering, "please, please dear, let me touch." you may have abandoned your flesh, sweet ghost, but i haven't.

i reach down between my legs and touch my clit. you can't take your eyes off my red nails as i start making little circles, slow and careful. watch me, girl, and when i let you, please follow. i spread my lips apart and slide a finger inside, and then i put my finger up to my mouth and replace my cigarette with the taste of my own wetness.

take my panties off for me, baby girl, pull them down with

your teeth and keep them there in your mouth. i want you to taste how wet you've already made me. you look fantastic with my panties in your mouth. you take a finger and place it right on my clit, exposed. i let out a little gasp—your fingertips have set my nerves on fire so quick. you make perfect little circles around it, you're such a tease. put your fingers inside me; i want you under my skin where you belong. where you have always been. push one finger in to test me out, then put the second and third in right away. push and pull me, play with me, rest your cheek on my inner thigh, and keep your eyes looking up.

my cigarette is burning down to the filter and warming my fingers. i kill the cherry and tell you to concentrate. you nod your pretty little panty-gagged face and pull your fingers out of me. my back is arched, my heels planted firmly on the ground. you are on your knees, between my sexy chubby thighs, pressing four fingers together and pushing into my cunt. one, two, three, four; you slide in so easily, my beautiful baby girl.

you're up to your knuckles in pussy and you're really starting to work it. you get deeper and deeper, never thrusting, only pushing farther inside. god, i've needed you inside me for so long. i only feel full when you feed me, i only feel satisfied when you're holding my heart in the palm of your hand in the centre of my wet, wet cunt.

my muscles are squeezing around you, pulsing like my heartbeats, just for you. my head is thrown back over the back of my chair, and i know the neighbours can hear my praise for you, my skilled apprentice. i feel as though i am about to melt around your wrist when you pause and command my attention with your eyes. i could overdose on those looks, for sure. without saying a word, without asking or needing permission, you spit my panties from your mouth and smile up at me. your hand stays still inside me as you bite my thighs. you bite hard enough to pull blood to the surface without breaking the skin. i am all shivers for you, my nipples hard as ice and pointing toward the sky, my face flushed, my body on the brink of climax—held prisoner in that delicate moment before explosion.

look up again and tell me you love me, baby girl, until i die. you know the recipe, you've mastered the spell. finish me off so that i may sleep in your arms forever, and wake from this dream that tortures my reality.

you follow a trail of bites home to my clit. you pull my clit up inside your mouth and suck on it as though i have a dick, and your fist enters me completely, finally filling me up. i let out the sweetest moans. you have my world in your hand. my ass lifts off the chair and my cunt pulls you so deep inside me it hurts. i am coming, spilling all over your hand, between your fingers, under your nails, down your wrist, in your sweet mouth, up your nose. my cunt won't let you go, i want you inside me forever, baby girl. you belong here.

instead, you disappear from the floor between my shaking thighs, and i find myself alone in my office, the computer light glowing off the slick sheen of sweat across my tits. i look at my own hand, drenched in come, and lick my fingers, wishing i was tasting myself on you. what would you do with me now, i wonder?

you're a phantom of desire, and you haunt me always. my lover, my wife, my best friend. where are you right now? what are you dreaming of under those soft eyelids, in that hot cave? i wish my screams were loud enough to wake you.

Shark

Kestrel Barnes

Queerspawn, that's what we are: me and Paul and Castor and baby Carling. Born and raised by dykes; we are one of the ways the Lesbian Nation reproduces itself. But some of us were also born of shark, some of us study sharks, some hunt for sharks and subdue them—all of us are scarred by shark. And we know that some dykes are sharks. They move through the world in human form, but they are sharks, no less.

My Mama studied sharks; basking sharks, great strong gentle sea creatures that raise their young in matriarchal groups. Sort of like some dykes do. I read that in my Mama's field journal. She was a marine biologist, a scientist who did her shark research in our backyard ocean.

"Just the facts, Ma'am," my Baba would tease her as she danced Mama around our kitchen, Paul and Castor balancing on her boots, me clutching her neck, all of us with our arms around one another, all of us together. We lived in an old summerhouse perched on an outcrop of rock overlooking the deepwater channel at Spencer Pass, way up in the fog-blown northwest rainforest. There were only a few houses scattered along the Pass, most of them inhabited by the coastal Native people who lived there long before Mama and Baba had moved there when the twins were small and I was still an unborn spawnling.

They'd met at a women's shelter in the Big Smoke—Baba was a support worker, Mama a grad student and a client. "Theory meets reality," they joked, though I never really knew who was supposed to be one or the other.

"Your Mama saved me," Baba always insisted, but it was Baba who stood down the man who hurt Mama and sent him away from us forever. Baba believed then that justice conquers violence. I now know that justice doesn't exist in nature or for those not bound by law, and sometimes not even for those who are.

"Anyway, Baba is our dad, our real dad," Paul always told me.

Baba took care of us while Mama studied. When I was almost three, Mama was immersed in her field studies of the basking sharks that fed near the beaches and coves of our stormy coast. She started catching glimpses of another creature that summer, something that was not supposed to exist in our waters, an interloper or anomaly of nature. Something that couldn't be real, except that it was. *It's an oceanic white tip shark,* she'd written after weeks of observation and research:

> May 28—Basking shark neonatal carcass washed up on Cripple Creek spit. Flesh wounds consistent with large predator attack (orca? shark?).
>
> June 2—M-pod orcas sounding and hunting off Home Bay site—observed shark dorsal fin in midst (blue/grey, white striped dorsal). Orca pod agitated, observed from 14:40 hrs until 15:05 hrs. No further shark dorsal fin sighted.
>
> June 5 —Spencer Pass channel 19:25 hrs. Observed mature sea lion being followed by white striped dorsal fin (shark?). Sea lion yanked below surface at 19:27 hrs.

June 6—Basking shark matriarchal group #51 in
Home Bay swimming in circles around #51 calves—
white tipped dorsal fin observed about 200 metres
out. What's going on here? No indigenous species of
shark fits this description.

June 10-12—(University of Victoria Marine Library)
studied shark species sighting reports for region
(1922–present); no sharks fitting description record-
ed. Three great white shark sightings near Queen
Charlotte Islands—could this be an atypically
marked great white?

June 15—Kokum Bear (SkyBear's grandmother) told
me a story she'd heard from the elders about a fearsome white marked shark that attacked a Haida war
canoe (1840s?) and devoured seven men. During the
next few days two more canoes were attacked, eight
more people killed in the water. Haida observed
shark hunting off Home Bay for an entire summer,
forcing them to move to Storm Bay fall camp two
months early. Kokum B remembers seeing a totem
pole commemorating the sea beast erected at old fall
camp.

June 17—Cripple Creek spit 18:35 hrs—grey-blue
dorsal fin circling seal colony, observed shark (ten
metres)—not a great white. (If not a great white,
what is it?)

It was her sighting again of that dorsal fin circling just starboard
of our dock that led to everything that came after.

We'd been to town for supplies and library books. Mama had
insisted that Baba stay home and rest on her one day off from
working the Crisis Line. Mama was always making sure Baba

didn't work too hard. She lovingly ironed her shirts and whispered sweetness into her blushing ears. And Baba could make Mama laugh and cry and sing all at the same time—I heard them many nights. On that night as we drove down the hill toward home, Mama caught sight of that thing again—the fin cutting the surface of the water. She drove out onto our dock, headlights streaming through the fog, searching for the flash of white on grey on sea-ink blue. Baba heard us arrive. She stepped out onto the widow's walk at the top of our house and called out, "I missed you, my love."

"Come and get the children," Mama called up to her. "I'm staying down here with the shark for awhile. Love you ..." And before Baba could reply, "Love you, too" (though Paul insisted that Baba had said it and Mama had heard her), the dock buckled and our truck slipped into the deep.

Baba howled as our truck sank. She was at the dock, ripping off her leather jacket and plunging in, before our truck sank below the surface. She pulled me out first and flung me onto the dock. Paul was next, his small body twisted at the waist. He crawled on his elbows to find me in the dark. It took a long time to free Castor from the tangle of car seats. Baba was heaving as she dragged him to the surface, but Castor wasn't breathing. Paul said that Baba paused in the water for a heartbeat, staring desperately below before climbing onto the dock with Castor limp in her arms. She smacked Castor on the back while he spewed sea water, then blew air into his sodden lungs. She implored, demanded, prayed, "Breathe, son, breathe." The moment Castor drew a breath, she jumped back into the water and dove again and again and again, trying to free Mama.

SkyBear said his dad heard Baba's howls that night, but Bear Senior maintained it was the truck's headlights bouncing off the ocean floor onto his front window that roused him. By the time our neighbour arrived to investigate, Baba was storming back from the dockside tool shed, a crowbar in her belt and a hacksaw in her hand. Baba decked SkyBear's dad with her bare fist, all 250 logger-muscled pounds of him, when he tried to stop her from cutting Mama free.

Baba must have known Mama was dead by then, dead before the truck even settled into the sea bed, dead before she knew her children were saved, dead with her feet crushed and ankles trapped in the truck's twisted front end. What we know and what we believe sometimes do not correspond. Maybe Baba couldn't go home without her, couldn't leave her love trapped in the deep, couldn't face us kids without bringing Mama to us. So while we huddled on the dock with her leather jacket protecting us, and as SkyBear's dad groaned back to consciousness, Baba hacked and cut Mama's feet off at the ankles and brought her body to the surface. Then dove twice more and freed the bits of bone left in her boots, and brought her—maimed, but all of her—back to us.

Baba rocked Mama's body in her arms and crooned sorrow into her unhearing ears. Castor wetly inhaled and exhaled, staring straight up at the stars. Paul's legs were twisted under him at an impossible angle. I clutched Baba, my cheek pressed against Mama's belly, staring down at her mangled legs. Mama's bones, or the bits that jutted out from her ankles and poked jagged from her boots beside her, were yellow. Not the yellow of fresh-churned butter or new-hatched chicks or the colour that played across our kitchen walls when the sun burned bright in summer, but more like the shade of the empty eggshells you find outside the hen house when the raccoons or foxes get there before you do. Or like the yellow-grey of a pearl you choke on and almost swallow.

She didn't bleed much, just two small pools draining out onto our dock, and some red fluid mixed with sea water sloshing out of her mangled boots. It didn't smell like the blood I knew—not the copper-and-kisses smell of skinned knees and Band-Aids. Mama's blood smelled like every promise you knew wouldn't ever be kept, like every secret that is revealed against your will. Her blood smelled just like the saddest tears, right before you cry. And her blood wasn't warm or cold I discovered when I reached down to touch the fluid seeping from her legs. It was the same temperature as the summer night air. Baba saw me touching the places Mama's feet should have been and she lifted my hand and printed Mama's blood onto her own chest just above her second shirt button. Then did the same for Castor and Paul. And then she placed the last smear of Mama's blood on my fingers against my chest and all of us were marked by Mama's blood and by her life and death, forever. And I lay back against Mama's belly and felt the warmth of her body slowly fade, each layer of skin releasing its heat into the darkness.

We were medevacked down to the Big Smoke by the harbour air ambulance. Baba refused to board until the zippered body bag was loaded in beside us. She held Mama's body and us all the way down to the hospital. What all the newspapers and local gossips described as a scene of unimaginable horror was just Baba's way of keeping our family together.

I found a picture in Mama's sea chest that was taken at the cemetery where we cremated her. Baba was wearing her best suit and the last white shirt Mama ever ironed for her. Her shoulders were rigid with grief, arms around Castor, whose head drooped and eyes stared vacantly. Paul sat in an oversized wheelchair, eyes burning. Both boys were in their little suits, ties neatly knotted by Baba, me tucked into her jacket, purple velvet dress scrunched up over my skinned knees, smiling solemnly. When Castor and, later, Paul were discharged from the hospital, we came home to scatter Mama's ashes off the dock and begin our life together without her. I barely remember those first months after Mama died. But I do remember the ten years we all lived together after that, before the shark came again.

Castor started to walk again, then run and fish and swim. But he never learned to write in anything but a precocious six-year-old's neat block printing, or read much beyond the books he'd sounded out for Mama. When, in the sixth grade, Paul tried to help Castor study for a history test, he prompted, "'The cliffs of Dover held archers, bows flexed, and as the enemy landed, the sea turned crimson.' Come on, Castor, answer the question, why did the sea turn red?"

Castor pondered cause and effect. "Shark attack?" Castor finally offered.

We stopped trying to teach Castor schoolwork after that, and just let him learn how and what he wanted. And though he never graduated, he could name all the plants and animals in the rainforest and all the sea creatures in the tide pools. He could navigate his sailboat by starlight and catch and clean fish for our dinner and chop enough firewood to keep us warm all winter. His eyes were content with all that needed to be forgotten.

Paul's broken back healed, but he never walked again. Baba carried him everywhere at first, with me balanced on her other arm. She built ramps to the porch and dock and beach, and Castor helped her renovate the house for Paul's wheelchair. Paul's mind was as quick as his body was broken, and he devised engines to power his beach buggies, and he mapped and plotted every trail he blazed. He could reason and debate, and he read his way through Mama's library and Baba's too. His eyes burned with the need of remembering.

I ran bare-chested through all our childhood summers. It seemed like me and SkyBear, whose mother wasn't around either, were always dogging the twins, building sand forts and scavenging the beaches for treasure, raiding the rainforest for wild berries, fishing off our dock and staying up late to watch the moon rise out of the ocean. Through all those long rain-lashed winter evenings we'd toast bread and cheese over the woodstove and snuggle under blankets while Paul read to us; we'd listen to the fog horns mourning when he paused to turn a page.

Baba dedicated herself to caring for us, to being our mother and dad, both. It's not like Baba never had any female companionship during those years. She'd sometimes pack her duffle bag and head out to the Big Smoke, or Seattle, or even back East. Sometimes she went to leatherfolk gatherings, sometimes to feminist conferences, often just for a night at the opera or a night at the bar.

"My lost weekends," she called them, dragging herself home with lipstick smears on her shirt collars, leathers and suits smelling of cigar smoke and strong liquor and some lady's perfume.

Whenever I asked her if she had a girlfriend she'd just laugh it off and dance me around the kitchen, saying, "Nah, you're my best girl." I think Baba closed her heart to loving anybody but us, for many years after Mama died. I know it wasn't love she was looking for when she went off for her weekends because when we were older and they didn't think I was listening, I once heard Paul ask Baba, "Are you going whoring?"

Baba didn't tell him to watch his mouth, but looked at him like you'd look at another adult, and answered him like he was a grownup. "Well, I call it hunting. Yeah, I'm going down to the bar next weekend."

"What's it like, to bare yourself to a stranger?"

"Well, the women I like do most of the baring, and they think I'm the stranger. Sometimes it's like growling into the void: you can feel the past erased and have nothing etched on the future. That's really all I want, just to take something for myself in the moment. But maybe it's just all I can bear."

"Can I come with you?" Paul asked, just as serious as she was.

"You're a bit young for it, boy. When you're older I'll introduce you around," Baba promised him. They shook hands, all solemn, then laughed and hugged each other.

It's not like I didn't know that Baba dated women. So I wasn't really paying attention that summer when Baba went down to the Big Smoke weekend after weekend, returning late, grinning and looking pensive at the same time. I had my own adventures—me and the twins and SkyBear had finally found his cousin's secret pot patch in the woods and we were busy stuffing our pockets and our pipes. And I'd spent most of the summer hanging out at the lake campground, playing ping-pong and swim-racing with the summer kids. I'd even kissed a girl that year, though she said she was just practising for when she got a boyfriend. So I really wasn't paying attention to Baba's affairs. It certainly never occurred to me that Baba was romancing a shark. But a shark she was, I discovered the first time I met her.

That Sunday Baba returned home early. From the widow's walk at the top of the house I watched her help some lady down from our truck. She took Baba's arm and strode assertively up the porch ramp, her stiletto heels clacking against the wood. She looked with disdain at our house, scraped a pointy fingernail over the weathered cedar siding and waited, tiny nose wrinkled, for Baba to open the front screen door for her. She acted like she owned the place, and Baba.

"Brooke, I'd like you to meet my daughter, Lambeth. Lamby, this is my girlfriend Brooke."

"That's Brooke with an 'e'," she directed.

"Uh, there's no 'e' in brook," was all I could think of to say.

"There is in my name, so don't you forget it." I stared into the eyes of a shark. Not a woman with sharky eyes, but a real shark. The room stayed the same, and so did Baba and the view outside our window, but Brooke had turned into a shark. I could smell her, an oily crushed reek overlaid with rotting guts exuding air-drowned puffs from her gills. Her grey-white skin stretched taut over cartilage, fins and tail flexing. Teeth bared in limitless hunger. Murky black shark eyes, reflecting nothing, fixed on me. I fled from the room, from the house, from my childhood, and hid in the forest.

Baba came looking for me at sundown, and I let her find me. "Oh Lamby, I'm sorry that this seems like such a sudden change.

I've been meaning to bring Brooke home for some time now. I didn't think you would be so upset." Baba cradled me in her arms with her leather jacket wrapped around us both, just like she had done when I was little and needed comforting. "Brooke is going to have a baby and I've asked her to move in with us. I was hoping that maybe you and Brooke would like each other," Baba said to me.

"Do you like her?" I asked. "Or do you love her like you loved Mama?"

Baba looked uncertain, like she had gotten lost in a fog patch and couldn't find her way out. "Lamby, your mother was the only woman that I ever loved with all my strength and all my soul and she loved me right back. And I never thought I'd want to love like that again or let anyone else love me. But I think I want to try, with Brooke. She needs a home and family. It will be good for us to have some femme energy in the house again. You and the boys might like it. I know I do." And though I was filled with foreboding, I promised Baba I would give Brooke a chance.

The shark moved in with us. She got started right away, whipping Baba and us into her version of what we should be. Rearranging furniture. Asking Baba to buy her new things. Like a shark agitating an orca pod, she stirred up our home.

She was a shark that only I could see. No one else seemed to notice the fishy smell, either. Well, she wasn't always a shark, sometimes she was just a shallow and demanding woman. She'd been some kind of child-protegé dancer and had won some big international scholarship way back when. Now she was supposed to be a choreographer, but she just seemed to spend her time leafing through magazines, talking on the phone with her friends, and criticizing anything that moved. I guess early accolades need to be backed up by mature work, but Brooke seemed to think that her job was to be dissatisfied, instead of writing dances.

Brooke even wanted to toss out Mama's sea chest. "Why are you keeping this smelly old box?" she questioned. Baba explained that it contained some of Mama's things, and that it was mine, for when I was older. Brooke had me drag the chest up to my bedroom, out of her sight.

The boys did their best to help her feel at home. Paul spent hours reconfiguring a computer for her, and he pretended not to care when she didn't thank him. Castor shyly brought her fresh-caught rock cod and spring salmon, which she ate all by herself, greed moistening her painted lips. She became frantic when she didn't get the best and biggest portions of whatever Baba cooked for dinner. She used her pregnancy as an excuse for her voracious need to feed. Baba deferred to her on everything. All Brooke would have to do was flash her toothy smile or pout a bit and Baba would agree to just about anything.

I wondered what would make someone into a shark, so I asked Paul about it. He knew an awful lot and nothing seemed to scare him. He knew where he was going in life. "An out-port cripple with a high GPA? I'm going to get skookum scholarship bucks." This was Paul's plan. Paul told me that the world was divided into predators and prey—everyone was one or the other. He wasn't too clear on what would turn a person into a predator. He thought it might have something to do with hunger, or wanting something and not caring what it cost, or maybe it was about preying for the sheer pleasure of the hunt.

"What are you?" I asked him.

"I haven't decided yet."

"What is Baba?"

"She's a good catch."

I didn't dare ask him about Brooke.

I read all through Mama's field journal, hoping that she'd written something, *anything*, about a shark-woman, but all her notes were on sharks that stayed sharks. I missed Mama whenever I opened her sea chest to read her field journal, or looked at photos of us all when she was still with us, or stroked her leather jacket.

I learned that sharks don't care for their young. Most women around Spencer Pass have their babies at home, with their mother and sisters and SkyBear's old Kokum helping out, so I knew about babies getting born. Brooke had a positive hatred of childbirth. "Just knock me out with drugs until it is all over," she demanded. She and Baba went down to the hospital in the Big Smoke. Baby Carling was sawed out of Brooke's belly, born in a pool of arterial blood. Of shark, but not a shark.

I tried to hate little Carling, really I did. I wanted to ignore her and reject her, but I couldn't. She was just so tiny and trusting. She couldn't help it if her mother was a shark. And just like a shark with a newborn pup, Brooke seemed to want little to do with Carling. She put me in charge of caring for the baby when Baba was away at work. Brooke spent more time complaining, in lengthy phone calls to her friends, about the trials of mothering us.

I'd been scared that Carling would be born a shark, but she wasn't, I soon satisfied myself of that. Her eyes were green as the tidepools and filled with life. Her mewls held no menace, her mouth was toothless and birdlike. She smelled like the rainforest after it rained. She couldn't swim, not in the bath, where I carefully examined her—no fins, no gills, no cartilage, and no tail. After that I knew for sure that Carling wasn't a shark. She was just my little sister.

I wondered if maybe Brooke had come from a family of sharks, but when I met Brooke's mother at the wedding I could see that she certainly wasn't a shark, just a carefully dressed church lady who looked a bit stunned by all the commotion. Baba and Brooke got married the summer of Carling's first birthday. Castor and Paul were the best men, dressed in their new best suits, ties knotted neatly just like Baba had taught them. I carried Carling who carried the ring. Fussed up, both of us were, in the matching purple crushed velvet pageboy outfits that Brooke made us wear when I'd refused to wear a dress. Baba took out her old best suit and shirt and bought a brand new wedding tie.

"Iron your own damn shirt," Brooke sniffed. So Baba did and she ironed some of Brooke's things, too. Baba didn't see the shark circling; she only saw her beautiful bride wearing a glittery wedding dress and satin stilettos. Their wedding was the best party this side of paradise, most of the guests agreed. All of Baba's (and even some of Mama's) friends came—a convoy of leatherdykes roared up the coast on their motorcycles, Birkenstock-clad Volvo-driving feminists arrived, all the fishing and logging families from miles around, and all of SkyBear's relatives came to our house for the festivities. I remember the tiniest femme leatherdyke licked SkyBear's dad at arm wrestling and made him say "aunt" to a girl. SkyBear's Kokum and aunts and some of the other women cooked and baked and cleaned and decorated far into the night. The meanest looking leatherdyke sobbed into a handkerchief all through the wedding service.

Brooke's friends came too—artists and musicians and writers. A whole minibus full of boy dancers arrived from San Francisco (they stayed downstairs with Paul, I could hear them laughing and talking all night).

I have to admit that it was a beautiful wedding ceremony out there on our dock with the sun being swallowed up by the sea just as a full moon rose out of the horizon and eagles circled overhead. For one night everything was all right. The next morning Baba and Brooke took Carling and departed for their honeymoon touring the dance halls of Europe—revisiting Brooke's old glory days.

There were several extensions on their honeymoon, and many delays getting home. By the time they returned, everything had changed. SkyBear left home and moved as far away as he could go. Paul had started university down at the Big Smoke. When I asked him if he liked it there and if he was making friends, he answered, "There's a wheelchair-accessible gay bar."

Soon after Castor shacked up with a woman he'd just met; they were living up in the bush. "What does that boy know about women, and what does she see in him?" Brooke grumbled. She refused to join Baba when she hiked up to visit them. Baba got home before dark, looking thoughtful. "Castor is where he wants to be. Let's be happy for them."

I hoped Castor was happier than Baba seemed to be. Baba didn't dance around our kitchen anymore. There weren't any giggling children hanging off her, and Brooke just pushed her away, sneering about her two left feet. Her shirts went un-ironed; Brooke wouldn't even drop them off at the drycleaners on her frequent trips to town. The only domestic task Brooke relished was the nightly ritual she'd imposed on us before bed, when she would make us all mugs of hot chocolate. It always tasted like curdled cream. And I never drank more than a sip before I'd dump it down the toilet on my way to bed. I began to lock my door at night. I swear somehow the shark would still slip into my room when she thought I was asleep and circle my bed. I dreamed of shark and woke to shark. It got so it seemed almost normal.

In all that time the shark lived with us it seemed that I was the only one it eyed with menace and bared its teeth to, until Baba finally stood up to Brooke. One evening, Baba announced at dinner, "Castor and his girlfriend need something of their own. I'm going to give them the woodlot with the cabin. Guess I should put both their names on the deed." Brooke started circling the table, screaming horrible accusations that Baba cared more for strangers and idiots than for her own wife. "Castor belongs in an institution," she snarled. "I should be half owner of our house and the woodlots. Put my name on the deeds, you bastard."

Some sharks can pursue their prey for days. Brooke fought with Baba and just wouldn't let it go. Baba tried to reason with her, tried to explain that all the children, even Carling, should have a share of the property she'd bought with Mama's insurance money, that Brooke too had a share, that we all owned everything together, and everyone would be provided for. The louder Brooke screamed and the filthier her accusations, the quieter Baba became, and the more insistent she was that Castor and his partner would have their woodlot.

Finally, Baba silenced Brooke. "I'm going to town next week and have the lawyer draw up the papers. I'm going to do the right thing for our family, for all of us. And that's the way it's going to be."

The shark, which had been circling us, locked its eyes on Baba and bared its teeth. I yelled "Watch out!" and they turned and looked at me.

The shark flickered in and out of existence, it opened its mouth to devour Baba and then it was just Brooke, who squeezed out a tear and changed her tune like you flip the dial on a short-wave radio. Suddenly she was sweetness and reason, agreeing that everyone should have a share, apologizing to Baba, enticing her upstairs to smooch and make up. I put Carling to bed, sang her every lullaby I knew, and tried to ignore the sounds I heard coming from Baba and Brooke's bedroom.

Too worried to sleep, I stayed up late looking through Mama's old sea chest. Brooke slipped into my room again and caught me wearing Mama's leather jacket and hugging its empty sleeves. I braced myself for more yelling, but instead she offered me her nightly cup of hot chocolate. "I'm sorry you've had to see all this fighting," she said sweetly. "Baba and I won't be fighting anymore. Now drink up, I made it especially for you." Brooke watched me with her shark eyes until the mug was nearly empty and I had laid my head on the pillow.

When I woke up in the middle of the night my head felt stuffed with fluff and fog. I tried to get out of bed and stumbled. It felt like an anchor was chained to my legs. I felt nauseous, seasick.

I dragged myself out into the hall and down to Carling's room. I couldn't wake her. She breathed shallowly and her eyes were rolled back when I lifted her lids. Panicked, I lurched up the stairs to rouse Baba to help me, but she wasn't there. Instead I found an overturned room, furniture knocked about, her boots and jacket kicked under the desk, some blood on the floor, the stench of shark everywhere.

I stepped out onto the widow's walk and saw Brooke, clipping up the dock in her stilettos dragging something burdensome and unwieldy. It was Baba, and I thought she was dead. I shook the sleep from my body and stumbled outside in the darkness down to our dock. "No," I yelled, catching Brooke off guard just as she had dragged Baba's body to the far edge. But she was only surprised for a moment.

"Did you want to attend your Baba's suicide? I thought that mug of hot chocolate would keep you asleep," she said, calmly and coldly.

"Baba isn't going to commit suicide. That's a lie."

"Her suicide note is on her computer. Too bad you won't get to read it. And it's your fault that now it will be a double murder-suicide." I shook my head, infuriated, as she spoke. "It doesn't matter what's true, it only matters what people believe. And they'll believe me. And every last thing of yours will be mine." She must have thought I'd cower as usual. But with Mama's leather jacket sleeve covering my arm, I clenched my fist and decked her, sending her backwards into the water.

She surfaced slowly and made some feeble splashing motions. Her hair clung to her face like seaweed. Blood gushed darkly from her nose into the moonlit water. I waited for her to turn into a shark, but she didn't.

"Lamby, help me," she pleaded in an all too human voice. I wanted to leave her in the ocean and let her sink with the weight of her own wickedness. But as I turned away from her I caught sight of something surfacing out in the channel. A huge shark, white-tipped fin slashing through the water, was circling toward Brooke. I don't know if the shark was drawn by Brooke's blood, or by her stilettos sparkling and churning against the tide. As the shark stalked her, it was almost as if it recognized her odour and knew Brooke was of its kind. And no matter what Brooke had done, no matter who she had hurt, I just couldn't leave her to that fearsome shark. I threw her the dock life preserver.

The look of triumph on Brooke's face as I began to haul her in scared me more than all her transformations. For the rest of my life I'll wonder if I let go of the life preserver rope before the shark reached her or if it was Brooke who let go first, when she saw the shark. The shark bumped its nose against her, tugged at her feet, dragged its pectoral fin over her. It looked like the shark was trying to mate with her. Brooke arched her back and reached out her arms to the shark in a gruesome, watery dance. Then the shark seized Brooke just below the throat, crunching through flesh and bone, twisted its massive body around her, and dragged her underwater. Silence and a slick of blood on the water was all that remained. Only one shark surfaced, and it wasn't Brooke. It circled in front of the dock one more time. It looked up at me with unfathomable eyes and then it was gone, forever. I fetched Carling from her bed and lay down on the dock with her beside Baba, who was groaning back to consciousness. I covered us all with Mama's leather jacket.

Brooke's body was never recovered, but her feet, still encased in sodden stilettos, washed up on shore next morning. All the newspapers and local gossips declared that once again we had been caught in the depths of unimaginable horror. I never told anyone about the shark. It was just my way of keeping my family together.

All You Can Be

Mette Bach

Sal Miller woke up clear headed, eyes open, scanning the lines of the bunk bed above her. Its grid horizontal, perpendicular, suspending another private, Rachel (was it?), from Tucson (maybe). Everyone here at Fort Bliss went by last names only, except the ones the sergeant gave nicknames. Identities were niceties (where are you from? what kind of music do you like?) exchanged back in boot camp a long time ago. In the service, conversations were limited, a quality that had attracted Sal, initially, to the idea of an army career. She was not much for getting to know people, not interested, she told herself, but sometimes a fleeting thought would tell her that she was scared, scared of people and the words they spoke and the things they did.

She had enlisted not because she wanted to further the American Empire, but because she wanted, more than anything, to become an engineer like her father. She didn't like her father, but she liked the idea of building structures, of seeing her visions take shape. She liked the idea of changing the horizon. She liked to think about bridges and suspension, the challenges of gravity, the beauty of mathematics. Her teachers in high school, far away, had called her a genius, but she did not like that label. She liked calculus, trigonometry, drafting, in the same way, she supposed, that some people liked other people.

Scholarships had been offered but not full scholarships, and Sal did not know how to supplement them. She made the kinds of calculations she did not like—how many trees would she have to plant in a summer to make enough money to survive the Ivy League? How many sandwiches would she have to make behind a deli counter? Her teachers, trying to be helpful, suggested loans or getting her parents' support, but Sal never asked anyone for help.

Instead, she picked up a pamphlet and attended a recruitment meeting. The army offered (*offered*, as in "it would be our pleasure") physical, emotional, and educational advancement.

Now, here she was, awake at dawn, minutes before the alarm would sound and the entire barracks would collectively grumble and moan their way out of bed, into their camouflage and boots and into the field. Every morning started the exact same way. The privates stretched, ran five miles, and stretched again. They came back to their quarters, made their beds, shined their boots, stood at attention for inspection, marched to the dining hall, and ate breakfast. It was an Ayn Rand dystopia.

The alarm sounded. The collective eyes opened. Sal's daydreaming was interrupted by the sound of fifty-eight feet hitting the ground, lacing boots.

"Miller. Get up."

Sal tried to sit up, but could not. Her muscles were not cooperating.

"Miller! Get up!"

She tried rolling on her side, but that, too, did not work. She tried lifting her head, but there was a disconnect between what she told her body to do and what she could manage.

"Miller?"

"I can't move," she said.

"You'll make us late," Private Walker said.

"I'm not doing pushups for you, Miller," Private Harding added, hovering over Sal's bed. She ripped Sal's blanket off and grabbed hold of Sal's arms and heaved her into a sitting position. Sal's body fell limp, on its side, the force of her unbalanced weight hurtling her to the floor. Face first, she landed on the cold linoleum-covered concrete.

Walker gasped. "Go get the sergeant."

A crowd formed around Sal. She could not feel the many hands on her as a number of women lifted her back into her bunk, into her initial position.

"Call the nurse," one voice said.

"I think we need a doctor," said another.

Sal woke up again, this time in a hospital bed. She looked around, scanning for a window, a clock, a person, an indication of how she'd gotten there and how much time had passed.

She hadn't been alone since she left home. She ate, slept, dressed with the others, lonelier than she had ever been. Crowds made her anxious. Here, alone, in the austere room, absorbing the clinical smell, Sal tried to move her arm, but it wouldn't; tried to curl a finger, but it didn't; tried to turn her head, but it was impossible.

"That's quite the predicament you're in," the white-coated doctor said, opening the door. His clipboard clutched to his chest, he adjusted his glasses and pulled a wheeled chair close to her bed and sat down.

"What's going on?" Sal asked.

"You tell me," he said.

"I can't move."

"I see that." He adjusted his weight from one side to the other.

"Why?"

"I was hoping you could tell me that," his tone distant, calculating.

"How would I know?"

He reached into his chest pocket and pulled out a lighter. With a flick of his thumb, he held a flame. They both looked at it. He inched it closer and closer to her arm.

"What are you doing?" Sal protested.

"I think we both know what's going on here."

"And what's that?"

"Come on," he said, inching the flame closer and closer until she smelled the singe of her arm hair.

With a perplexed expression, the doctor let the flame go out. "Oh. You're not faking." He seemed disappointed.

"Faking what?"

"Paralysis."

"Why would I fake paralysis?"

"Why does anyone fake anything? Honourable discharge? I don't know. I have to rule everything out."

Sal wondered if she could change her circumstances with a change in attitude. If she expected this doctor to help her, would he? She expected him to irritate her, isolate her, bother her—and he did. In his hands she placed the fate of her body, which she no longer had control over. If she had control, she would have left the room, stopped listening. Men like the doctor frightened her.

"Yesterday you were fine, and today you wake up like this?"

"Yes."

Sal could not even begin to explain that her definition of "fine" and his might not be the same. In fact, her definition of "fine" might be vastly different from anyone in all of the barracks. How could she point out the awfulness of the entire situation to someone who seemed intent on disbelieving her?

"So you didn't do anything strenuous?" he inquisitioned her.

"Not especially."

The doctor left the room. Sal closed her eyes and imagined a window to look out of. Instead, she lay on a bed in a room of empty beds. George Orwell was a military man, wasn't he? No wonder he turned to fiction.

"You're being moved," the doctor said condescendingly. He was barely in the room before Sal felt sick. "Dr. Van de Kroop will take you in the Psychiatric Ward. It's psychosomatic, what you have."

"What are you saying?"

"It's in your head."

"I know what 'psychosomatic' means. When will I get better?"

"I guess that's up to you," he said, one eyebrow slightly raised, creating the appearance of confidence with a practised hint of concern.

Sal was moved to the Psychiatric Ward. Her bed was next to a window where she could look down each morning at her peers, still living the life of the six-a.m. runs.

Sal waited for a door to open. What a horrid metaphor when doors open to hallways like these—sterile, fluorescent, crisp. There are two kinds of people according to rooms like this: those who are psychologically balanced (professionals) and those who need their help (Sal). The door swung open and a long-haired woman breezed through, theatrical, caricature-like. She wore a lab coat over her power suit, which gave her an air of self-assurance. Sal had learned to be skeptical of women like her.

"I'm Dr. Van de Kroop, but you can call me Brianna." She stretched a long thin hand in Sal's direction.

Sal's limp body could not return the gesture.

"Oh, sorry, I forgot," Brianna giggled, nervous. "How are you today?"

"Paralyzed."

The moment was awkward. Brianna thought that Sal had made a joke, and so she laughed just enough to realize that she was alone in her laughter. She pulled a chair from one side of the room (where they kept dolls and yarn and puzzles) to Sal's steel bed.

"You seem cynical," Brianna said, perfectly poised with open body language, eye contact, and a perfunctory empathetic facial expression fresh from college.

"Cynical?" Sal wondered if she needed to remind her that they were in a military hospital, even though it did not look like one. Cynical. What a dumb assessment. Who isn't?

"I'm here to help you. Do you want my help?"

Sal's immediate (yet unuttered) response was *no*. Instead of saying anything, Sal thought about the question and its implication that Brianna *could* help. This seemed unlikely. Sal did not respond the way she thought she would.

"Yes, I want your help. I want to sit up and walk again."

"Then you're going to need to let me in here." She tapped her chest above her heart and nodded her head in what Sal gauged as a cheap attempt at manipulation. She did not nod back.

"I don't want to do that."

"But you want to get better."

"I want to take a piss by myself."

"That's better than where you're at right now, isn't it?"

Sal conceded that Brianna's logic was superior. Brianna was the kind of woman who displayed zeal in her work, who would gleefully chirp to the other therapists about the "progress" they were making. The very idea of it—of this dividing line, of Brianna "helping" her—sickened Sal.

"Why are you so resistant? We're trying to help you." Brianna flipped through Sal's file.

"I just want to be able to sit up. I wasn't supposed to be here, like this." Sal was frustrated by her body's betrayal, like being held captive within herself.

"Sometimes these kinds of things—hysterical paralysis in particular—manifest themselves to give you an opportunity to reconsider your path."

Sal had a low tolerance for New-Age mumbo-jumbo and could

not help but feel that Brianna had never had to reconsider her path. Outside these walls, Sal wouldn't speak to a woman like Brianna, but here they both were, doctor and patient. Once inside a psychiatric ward, one no longer has the freedom to debate diagnoses or the very construct of the sane helping the insane. Sal knew that her best strategy was to be amenable.

"What's going on for you?" Brianna urged, casually leaning against Sal's bed, looking at her over the frames of her glasses, her face tilted slightly downward in practised perfection.

"I can't move."

"And?"

"It's frustrating."

"What's going on for you emotionally?" Brianna asked. Sal knew she better pony up a better response and quick.

"I'm part of the machine," she said, consciously contemplative. "It doesn't matter that I don't have a gun on me. I'm a soldier. For that matter, so are you." Sal was impressed with the grace of her own rhetoric.

"I'm a therapist."

"We're both part of the machine." Her logic was swift. The dividing line between doctor and patient had happened fast—as these things do—as overnight she went from well to unwell. Brianna had to recognize the absurdity of this system she belonged to. It wasn't as simple as well and unwell. It couldn't be.

"Is that what this is about?" Brianna's eyes traced Sal's still body. "You see yourself as a soldier and you don't want to be one?"

"I don't 'see myself as a soldier,' I am one. Don't you get that?"

"Sal, you haven't even been in combat."

This postulation stung. Brianna's ignorant words were harsh and logical but false. Brianna claimed to want to help but seemed as though she had not given much thought to what the military actually did, what a life of service actually meant. Sal speculated that maybe this denial was why her body opted out. Perhaps on a cellular level, she knew she could not stay.

For weeks, the women spent most of their days together, focused on the project of Sal's recovery, and they made "great strides" according to Brianna's reports. Sal had come to understand herself through working with Brianna. She had learned to accept that her body had responded to stimulus she hadn't even been aware of. She opened up to Brianna, shared secrets as small as her breakfast cereal cravings and as large as her fear of never being good enough. They eased into conversations that felt impossible with anyone else. They had no trouble reprimanding each other.

"When we first met, you gave me the pretty-girl write-off." Brianna's tone was low, personal.

"The what? I don't know what that is." Sal found it arrogant of Brianna to refer to herself as pretty, even though it was true.

"You thought you knew everything about me based on what I look like."

"I didn't."

"Don't lie," Brianna said. "It's okay, though. I tried to give you the handsome-girl handshake."

"You did?" Sal's eyes widened. No one had called her handsome before, and it fit like her favourite track pants. "I don't know what that is either."

"Do I have to spell it out? I thought you were cute." Brianna smiled, shy, coy. When she avoided eye contact because of nerves, she was even prettier. There was something confident about the risk of her words. Sal had never been called cute, except as a child by her grandparents.

Brianna lifted the sheets from Sal's side, exposing the skin of her leg.

"Here," she said, reaching into her lab coat pocket, pulling out a syringe, "I'm going to give you an injection. It will stimulate your muscles. I want you to get better." Her voice was tender.

Sal felt cared for. Brianna's attention was lovely and flattering, and even though it was something Sal had not been used to, she felt like it was something that maybe she should get used to. Maybe people were not altogether as suspect as she had believed.

Over the weeks they spent together, Sal started to understand how she had isolated herself and how she could change. She trusted Brianna. She wasn't sure why, but it seemed impossible not to. Theirs was a symbiotic connection. Brianna confessed that she, too, had been alone, isolated, frustrated with human contact and interaction, unable to find solace in conversation.

"I feel like I can actually talk to you. I never feel that way," Sal said one afternoon.

"Can I ask you something? Are you a lesbian?" Brianna asked. She had a way of putting Sal on the spot like that, a trait that made her both alluring and frightening.

"I thought no one was supposed to talk about that. Don't ask. Don't tell."

"Maybe I'm not asking in a professional capacity." Brianna pulled her chair in close to Sal's horizontal body. Sal could smell Brianna's hair, a fresh herbal scent. She wanted to breathe Brianna's hair deep into her lungs, suffocate on her long brunette locks and be enveloped in that mane. Brianna rested her head, unprofessionally, on Sal's chest. They enjoyed the sound of each others' breathing.

"Do you believe in fate?" Brianna asked. "Do you think that maybe all this was meant to happen so that we could meet?"

Sal, who had always been an atheist and a practitioner of science, mathematics, and calculable randomness, heard her voice declare without hesitation, "Yes. I believe in fate."

"I really like you, Sal."

The phrase, like butter melting on toast, seeped into Sal.

"I like you, too, Brianna. Can I confess something? Part of

me wants to stay here with you forever, even if it means never walking again."

"Can I tell you something?" Brianna asked. "I want that, too."

"Can we stay in touch when I get better? What are your plans? Would you ever leave the military?" Sal's mind flooded with visions of the two of them. They were on horseback, riding through New Mexico, the sun beating down on their warm, free bodies. They were in Alabama, baking pie in their shared home that had once been a salvaged plantation-turned-organic-farm where they would renovate the land, maybe lobby to have it rezoned as park land. They were in Canada, signing papers, declaring their love, celebrating their marriage. All kinds of fantasies seemed possible.

"Of course I want to leave with you. Let's concentrate on getting you to walk again first," Brianna said, reaching into her coat pocket for the daily syringe that had become part of their afternoon ritual. "Don't be scared, Sal." Brianna placed the palm of her hand on Sal's arm, tender, light. Brianna radiated heat. Sal's skin burned hot like the Texas sun. A tiny prick, a cool puncture from the steel tip of the syringe, and Sal felt a refreshing stream trickle into her.

Brianna's hand was firm as she gave Sal the injection that allowed her to relax. She trusted Brianna. The extent of the trust was surprising. Perhaps it wasn't trust as much as tension, that she wanted the touching to go further, even as she resisted the desire. How plainly we self-censor, not wanting things that we are told we shouldn't want. Doctor and patient. Touching. Two military women. Touching. An introverted engineer and an extroverted counsellor. Touching. So wrong. So right.

"If you want me to stop, just say so," Brianna whispered as she lowered her face to Sal's, so close that Sal's whole body, though still, glowed like embers. Brianna's lips descended, closer and closer until the soft skin of her bottom lip touched Sal's top lip. Unstoppable, they pressed hard against each other, skin on skin, lips on lips, determined.

"I don't want you to stop. I don't ever want you to stop," Sal managed to muffle the words.

Brianna liked the sound of those words, her body lithe and warm next to Sal. She stopped, mid-kiss, and jolted toward the door. One quick turn of the lock, another pull of the curtain across the only window to the corridor, and a final flick of the light switch and the room was transformed. Brianna tossed her lab coat onto the empty bed beside Sal's.

Sal watched her with intensity. Being unable to move, Sal relied entirely on Brianna. She was desperate to touch Brianna. She had wanted that for a long time now, had thought of it often when Brianna rested her head against her chest. How infuriating that her body would not allow her to act on it.

"It's almost like bondage," Brianna teased as she stood next to Sal's bed and slowly undid the buttons of her shirt.

"Come back, let me kiss you," Sal pleaded.

Brianna straddled herself atop Sal's limp body. Sal could feel her deep inside and imagined being able to wrap her arms and legs around her. She wanted to cradle Brianna, hold her close and caress her skin. She cursed the blankets and paralysis between them even as she savoured every second of Brianna's presence on top of her.

Brianna enjoyed Sal's immobility. She liked playing. She liked controlling Sal's fate. She liked being so close to Sal's mouth that they were nearly touching and then pulling back just a little and watching Sal's disappointed expression. There was something powerful about being the object of Sal's affection. She enjoyed the vision of herself as unattainable. Near Sal, she felt like she could realize a part of herself that she longed for. She needed to be needed and Sal needed her in every way imaginable.

"Tell me how much you want me," Brianna urged. "Tell me

how badly you want to fuck me."

These words made Sal nervous. She saw herself as shy, a little awkward. It wasn't her style to speak her fantasies, even though she did want to fuck Brianna. But what did that mean? What did she know about fucking another person? She had never even kissed a girl before. She moaned, hoping that Brianna would delight in the pleasure of the sounds they made together and forget about words.

"I want to hear you tell me. Tell me I'm sexy. Tell me how badly you want to touch me," Brianna ordered, taking her shirt off to reveal a lacy bra. "Tell me you love the way my tits look."

Sal's palms sweated and she did everything she could to force the words out. "You're beautiful, Brianna. I'm lucky to be here with you."

"Yes," Brianna said, unhooking her bra, tossing it aside, "you are very lucky that I picked you to be my patient. You're my favourite, you know."

Sal soaked up the palpable currency of Brianna's words, like desert cacti thirsty for rain. All forms of desire she had experienced in her life became abstract in contrast to this very real longing. She wanted not just to feel Brianna's body against her own, she wanted closeness, the erasure of barriers, a sacred connection, which struck her as odd since she had not considered herself a believer. She believed in this. She wanted this.

"I'm going to help you fuck me," Brianna whispered into Sal's ear. She lifted herself up, positioning her breasts right in front of Sal's face. Sal instinctively reached her tongue out as far as it would go and licked Brianna's hard left nipple. Brianna tilted her head back and moaned with a delightfully low pitch, one that came from deep inside.

"I've wanted to feel your mouth on my nipples ever since I first saw you," Brianna said, looking toward the window through which she first saw Sal, many months earlier on the six-a.m. runs.

Brianna hiked up her skirt and balanced herself, holding onto the metal frame of the hospital bed, creating the perfect angle, positioning her raspberry nipples a sugary distance from Sal's lips. Sal's unmoving hand lay curled, just so, beneath the salt-watery moisture. Brianna shoved her nipple into Sal's mouth. Through sheer violet panties, Sal could smell and feel Brianna's wetness against her skin.

Both of them were breathing heavily, practically panting as Brianna slid Sal's limp hand into her panties, moving it back and forth against her wetness. Her eyes rolled into the back of her head, and she sighed with pleasure. Faster and faster she pumped Sal's hand, moving it back and forth against her clit.

Sal had not even known how to imagine sex, especially with Brianna. She watched her and listened to her moans, feeling almost envious that she would not be able to feel the same sensations. Brianna pumped Sal's hand over her clit, her speed and expression intensifying. Sal watched in disbelief as though her hand was someone else's, as though this was all happening in front of her, not because of her or with her. She held her breath with anticipation as Brianna arched herself backward, slippery with determination, and let out a cry that sounded painful. Brianna gasped for air, then crumbled, as though she had deflated, onto Sal's chest.

The two of them lay there together, Brianna clutching Sal, her heartbeat slowing to its usual pattern.

After what seemed like forever, Sal spoke. "Once I learn to walk again, I'm hoping to get a discharge. I want you to come with me when I leave. I want to make you happy, Brianna."

"You already make me happy," she countered.

"I have to concentrate on walking, on getting better, on getting out. Then we can get out of here. Right now everyone here thinks I'm crazy, hysterical."

"You're not crazy."

"You say that so effortlessly." Sal was flattered at Brianna's faith in her. "How do you know? How do any of us know?"

"It's my profession."

Against her better judgment and everything that Sal had learned to believe about love and intimacy and connection and attraction, she felt herself changing, opening. The layers of cynicism and solitude, layers she relied on, layers upon which she built her existence, were questionable. Brianna's mere existence put Sal's beliefs under scrutiny. Maybe she wasn't alone after all. Together, they could get out of this labyrinth, this maze of military horror. Together, they could start a new life.

Brianna dressed slowly as though she wanted to linger in the moment, savouring their union.

"Let me give you your injection before I go," Brianna said, pulling a vial from the pocket in her lab coat. Even in the dark, Brianna's control of the syringe seemed effortless and natural, as though giving inoculations was an extension of her very being.

The cold steel needle slid gently into Sal's side. It was delicate—a tiny prick followed by a tiny push, filling her muscles with the clear liquid that promised to stimulate. It was strange how medicine worked. With each injection, she found herself more relaxed, more limp, more reliant.

In the hallway, outside the closed door, the doctors gathered. It was the usual check-in, a team of superiors visiting Dr. Van de Kroop and everyone else at the ward. It was routine.

"How is this patient progressing?" The one with the clipboard gestured to the window in Sal's door.

"I'm afraid she isn't."

"Hmm. I would have thought that two months in intensive care would have done the trick."

"I thought so too, at first," Brianna said. "Now it looks like she might never walk again."

Here Lies the Last Lesbian Rental in East Vancouver

Amber Dawn

> *For Maz Sykes, and for anyone who has paid more than just rent to be at home.*

Trinket wrapped her arms behind her knees and buried her face between her thighs—as if bracing for a crash landing—a limber pose she only does when she's showing off, like the splits or the crab walk. But Trinket wasn't flaunting. She was delirious. She was drooling, crying, hyperventilating with emotional overload.

Her girlfriend Zoya stabbed at the ignition with her keys, missing once, missing twice. The third time she jammed the key in crooked and let out a frustrated groan. She sat back in the driver's seat to try and quiet her trembling hands with a few long, deep breaths. If she didn't relax she was bound to snap the key in the ignition, or be suffocated by her own corset, or both. "Breathe," she instructed herself out loud. She laid a hand on Trinket's back, urging her girlfriend's gasps to slow as well.

Under the street lamp's yellow glow, Zoya watched Trinket's ribs move with each inhale and exhale. Her boney spine looked like a rippled sand dune, the kind Zoya had only seen in photographs of Morocco or Death Valley National Park. The notion of driving all the way to the desert—any desert—popped into Zoya's head. They could go wherever they wanted, she thought as she successfully slid the keys into the ignition. They were alive.

And that ... thing ... inside the house definitely was not.

The house didn't stand; rather, it sat in a slumped-veranda, recumbent-rooftop position, two doors from the corner of Templeton and Sixth Avenue. No one bothered to notice exactly when the house began its weary way toward the earth, but once it had sunk it stayed that way.

In 1949 Guido Gambini's heavy black eyebrows touched as he squinted at the three-bedroom stucco bungalow salted in broken glass. Guido had never seen a broken-glass stucco before. He pondered the number of crushed wine bottles stuck to the exterior of his new home. He imagined the many people who had drunk from those bottles; picnickers cuddled under a cypress tree, large families who shouted across the dinner table. *This house will bring us many happy years*, Guido thought when he bought it.

Biba Gambini, a green-eyed Calabrian with a sturdier frame than her new Canadian house, was especially fond of the basement. It was her matronly citadel, her woman's fort. If she wasn't in the basement canning then she could be found in the garden, growing more vegetables to can. She stomped up and down the basement stairs so frequently Guido grew exhausted just listening to the booming sound of her steps. *If only she'd bring that kind of vigour into the bedroom*, he pined. Each night she slipped into bed smelling of damp earth, and promptly fell asleep.

Guido only descended into her domain on two occasions. During the first autumn of their marriage, he heard an awful crash below him and rushed to find his wife at the bottom of the stairs, half-buried beneath a heavy pine table. "We just had a wedding and now you want a funeral?" he asked, after he had her sitting upright again. "Why would you carry it? Down the stairs! By yourself! Do you not have a husband?"

"I need it for canning," is all Biba said. And indeed there were the many Mason jars along cellar shelves to prove her point. Before Biba shooed Guido back upstairs he gazed in gape-mouthed wonder at her canning cache. There were tomatoes, of course; Biba made sure there was no shortage of tomatoes. And canned beans; Biba had runner beans trained along the garden fence and cannelloni beans as early as May. Then there were the jars of food that puzzled Guido—chili peppers, marinated okra, octopus tentacles. Where was Biba getting this octopus? Guido never asked.

When Biba died of cardiac arrest before they saw their tenth anniversary, Guido visited the basement a second time to shout at the tomato sauce and cry to the oily octopus tentacles pressed against cylindrical glass.

He couldn't bear to sell the house any more than he could live in it. And after touring several pairs of newlyweds through the empty rooms, he decided against renting to young, rosy couples. Instead, he offered the keys to two women. They weren't old enough to be spinsters, but there was something about them— the way they folded their arms in front of their chests, jutted their chins out, and their perfume smelled more like chopped wood than florals—little clues that told Guido these women had no hope of finding husbands.

This was his landlord's strategy: rent to women. Countless stiff, seemingly chaste women. Otherwise, he paid no attention to the rotation of ostentatious paint colours, the untiring dance of Polyfilla and nail holes on the plaster walls, or anything else that happened in the house.

Zoya's mean mommy routine wavered slightly after Trinket said, "Thank you," and the corners of her carnelian red lips curled into an involuntary smile. She looked out the curtain-less attic window to prevent Trinket from seeing her gleeful expression.

Throughout most of their relationship Trinket had been a fount of thankfulness. If Zoya had a dollar for every time Trinket said "thank you," they could have bought themselves a house. Re-grettably, Trinket's good manners had zero monetary value, and the house she and Zoya lived in—where they first met, where for two years they fucked and shared food with friends and threw parties and fought and fucked some more—had recently been sold. Their notice of eviction soon followed. Ever since, Trinket hadn't felt very grateful. Rightfully put, her mood had been downright dismal. And so Zoya quietly drank in Trinket's "thank you" like water during a dry spell.

Both Trinket's wrists were hitched in black silk upholstery cord, bought specifically to match Zoya's brocade corset. Trin-ket had a theory that Zoya's fondness for coordinating their lin-gerie and personal effects had something to do with Zoya being an only child who was denied Barbie dolls and Bonne Bell make-up, and instead was made to read the works of ancient poets and philosophers such as Rumi and Horace. Trinket also suspected that this accounted for a fair share of Zoya's sadism.

The root of Trinket's nearly rabid devotion remained a big question. She certainly never saw it—meaning Zoya—coming. On their first date they went from kissing on a rainy Novem-ber beach to Zoya bending Trinket over a granite boulder and spanking her ass and pussy with her leather driving glove. "Is that your come on my new glove?" Zoya had thrust the sticky glove at Trinket's nose. Trinket's only response was giddy laugh-ter. Not amused, Zoya had Trinket walk back to the car with the glove crammed in her mouth. Trinket suckled and gagged, though she didn't protest. Her willingness surprised her. She had been willing ever since.

In their attic room, Trinket thanked Zoya for roughly one foot of the black silk rope. Rather than hog-tying Trinket's wrists tightly together behind her back, Zoya left a foot or so between each knotted cuff so Trinket had partial use of her arms. She reached back to touch Zoya, who stood ominously close behind her and said it again: "Thank you."

Zoya then bound her legs in a similar fashion: ankle cuffs with a couple of feet of rope between them. Trinket did not thank her for taking away her ability to spread her legs wide open. She entertained the idea of kicking her feet to mess up Zoya's knots. But if ever there was a night to be a good girl, this was it.

It was their last night in the house. All their belongings—apart from the stool, the rope and whatever surprises Zoya had brought in her black briefcase—had already been moved to their new apartment.

"Remember how this attic room used to give you the creeps?" Zoya asked. "Now, after all this time, tell me the truth, that was an excuse to get into my bed, wasn't it?" Before they were lovers they were roommates. They're queer. It's East Vancouver. It happens.

"This room is drafty," Trinket complained about her old bedroom.

"The whole house is drafty," said Zoya. Ever since the house had sold, Zoya had been quick to point out its shortcomings. Testy wiring topped her list. "Think of how many times we reset the clocks. All the surge protectors in the world won't help this house." And Banjo, their Boston terrier, always managed to escape through some unseen door in the middle of the night to bark hysterically in the back yard. And the taps dripped … the list went on.

"At least it's quiet here," moped Trinket. "There's so much traffic and construction on Main Street."

"Oh, it's quiet here, hmm?" Zoya said as she grabbed a fistful of Trinket's hair. Trinket squealed. "It doesn't seem so quiet to me." Trinket lowered her squeal to the baby-girl baying she knew Zoya was fond of hearing. Zoya yanked her head back to slip a blindfold over her eyes. That was what the slack foot of rope was for, Trinket suddenly realized. Zoya had bound her hands just tight enough so she wouldn't be able to remove the blindfold.

Darkness had never become a matter of course for Trinket. The blindfold still rattled her as much as it had their first time using it. Likewise, Zoya never tired of watching Trinket jerk and twist, reaching helplessly around her for something to grab onto.

"Stay on your perch, little one." Zoya warned. Trinket squirmed on the stool as she heard the metallic snap of the brief-case opening. An assortment of clonks and jangles sounded in Trinket's ears as she tried to guess which toys where being set out. She hoped to hear the happy clanking of the metal buckles on Zoya's harness. Instead there were seemingly long silent gaps with only the windy whir that the house always made, now amplified throughout the empty rooms. Occasionally Zoya tapped something on Trinket's kneecap or shoulder, but the touch was too brief for Trinket to guess what was rubber and what was leather.

"You know, I don't mind a noisy house, as long as the noises are yours." Zoya picked up the thread of their last conversation, which, to Trinket, felt like an eternity ago. She stuck two fingers into Trinket's mouth, and Trinket found herself automatically moaning and suckling. "So eager tonight, and I haven't even gotten started with you yet." Zoya pushed her fingers further into Trinket's mouth, hooked them around her bottom row of teeth, and pulled Trinket's face to her breasts. Zoya let her rest there, allowing Trinket to nuzzle into her for a quick second before taking a sudden step back. Trinket lost her balance, as Zoya knew she would. The floorboards squeaked unapologetically beneath her as she floundered to right herself on the stool again. At 5'1", any barstool was a reach for Trinket, and Zoya had purposely picked the tallest one. She laughed a little at Trinket's blinded loss of equilibrium. Then, in a flash of ruthlessness, she wound up her leather boot and swiftly kicked the stool out from under Trinket. It hit the far wall with a terrible crash. Trinket screamed and laughed like mad, nearly toppling over.

"I'll give you ten whole minutes to hide," said Zoya, gravely. Trinket scrambled forward a few steps before an arm wrapped around her waist. Her legs kept moving on the spot like a marionette.

"How many minutes did I generously give you?" Zoya asked.

"Ten minutes," Trinket huffed. "Ten generous minutes."

"Well then, there's no need to go tripping down the stairs, is there?" Despite this warning, on Trinket's next step she walked headlong into the doorframe. The mild blow shook her confidence. She was tempted to lie down on the floor in a "game-over" fetal position. *You know this house*, she reminded herself, *with your eyes closed. Don't let it defeat you.*

Before her was the staircase. She ran her toes over the top step, twisted awkwardly to grab a hold of the banister, then sidled down the stairs one careful step at a time.

When she reached the main floor she smelled paraffin. Under the rim of the blindfold she spied candlelight and was drawn to it like a moth. Melted wax spilled on Trinket's toes as she accidentally tipped a votive candle with her foot. *It's nearly impossible to get wax off of an old hardwood floor*, Trinket thought as she mashed the hot wax into the floorboards with bare feet: a present for the new owners. She traced the room and found dozens more candles along the baseboard. She left them upright, knowing Zoya probably laid them out to keep her from walking into walls.

The living room used to be an obstacle course of overflowing bookshelves, armchairs crowded with throw pillows, and a jungle of houseplants in the bay window. Once, during a similar game, Trinket zipped herself into a duvet cover and burrowed into their nest of a sofa. Zoya had stormed the house searching for her. Hide-and-seek was their favourite foreplay game. With all her hiding places gone, Trinket wandered in blind circles from the living room to the kitchen, the den, and back again. She made a desperate attempt to tuck herself under the kitchen sink, but the drainpipe refused to move over to let her in.

She stood at the back door for a while, wrestling the doorknob with her rope-bound hands. Finally the door cracked open and June night air rushed in, making her shiver. Trinket imagined evening dew against her skin. She figured it was all right to be outside naked and blindfolded, since they wouldn't be sticking around to face the neighbour's reaction in the morning. She stepped through the door onto the prickly straw doormat. A few more steps and she found grass beneath her feet.

Over the years, the Gambini back garden was dug up and re-sown with every manner of flora imaginable. Vegetables continued strong through the 1960s, although the first tenants allowed dozens of zucchini to overripen on the vine. Slugs dined on the basil and the mint. And not a single tomato was blanched and canned.

An assembly of sunflowers rang in the next decade, and the yard became a supper club for hungry sparrows and squirrels. Those were crooner days, the early '70s. Passersby might have heard Barry Manilow or Wayne Newton lyrics being sung in lullaby voices. If one were to have peeked over the garden fence, one would have seen women serenading each other, a record player propped in the open back window.

But there was no holding back "Skyrockets in flight, afternoon delight" on eight-track cassette. Soon enough the sunflowers petrified on their stocks, and the whole, poorly-tended lot was strangled by creeping morning glory, which, by chance, was the perfect weedy bed for a group Quaalude and make-out trip.

Bonfires burned for the better part of the '80s. Marshmallows browned as impromptu direct-action groups were formed. Anti-poverty, anti-war, anti-Expo, anti-fur, anti-cruise-missile-testing, and anti-industrial protest signs were constructed in the basement. After the sit-ins and marches were finished the same signs were burned in the fire pit to destroy the evidence.

Anne Goldstein, anti-violence activist, feminist collective founder, and tenant from 1981 to 1985, named the house the Fire Brigade after the 1982 anti-porn firebombings of three local Red Hot Video stores.

The next tenants kept the house name but built a skateboard half-pipe over the fire pit. The tenants after that flooded the yard and started a lesbian mud-wrestling federation—Team Fire Brigade held the title of tag-team champions for two consecutive summers.

In the millennium, the house was rechristened the Crotch Fire Brigade, which would have had the '80s second-wave feminists cringing with disgust. The polyamorous, pomosexual renters transformed the yard into an underground, vintage porn-viewing gallery. Bed sheets were tacked to the house and cast with grainy black-and-white nudes. The projector sat on a dumpstered card table that often collapsed, throwing the lurid images into the night sky. This never really bothered the audience; they kept themselves busy inside their sleeping bags while the projectionist fussed with table legs and reels of film. It was the first time in thirty years old Guido Gambini had to give his tenants a noise complaint warning.

In August 2004, Trinket Campbell bought a wheelbarrow's worth of sod and introduced the back garden to something completely different: grass. Each day, for weeks, she stood outside with the garden hose and watered the grass to root. Not much later, Zoya Feiz would tell stories about how she fell in love with the impish girl with muddy bare feet and a soaking wet sundress standing in her own backyard.

Trinket's feet pressed into the damp earth. Outside there weren't any walls to stub her toes on. She imagined grass tickling her back, mud on her knees; she wanted to get her hands dirty.

More than this she wanted to experience whatever Zoya had in store for her, and she appreciated that Zoya wouldn't want her best corset, her stiletto boots, and other fetish finery ruined in the dirt. "Where can I hide?" she asked herself, turning back toward the house. A warm glow caught her attention, and although she couldn't see exactly where the light was, after stumbling several steps toward it she guessed it was coming from the basement window. Had Zoya set up a play scene in the basement? "For the love of fuck," Trinket said to herself. The basement creeped her out more than the attic could ever hope to.

Her fear was largely Zoya's fault—whenever something needed to be done down there Zoya would chime in with tales of spiders and bats and loose murderers hiding under the stairs. Trinket gave over easily to the power of suggestion; sometimes she would actually hear noises. Batwings? The sharpening of a blade?

Even before Trinket moved in she had heard stories about the basement at the Fire Brigade. The rumour most frequently churned around the gossip mill was that an old widower had killed his wife, thrown her down the stairs during a lovers' quarrel. There were reddish stains on the concrete floor that never washed off, as if to prove it. When Trinket met Guido—the gentle-faced man wringing his meaty hands as he collected the rent—she discarded those horror stories as pure fiction.

Many a story was told about the Fire Brigade; who knew anymore what was true and what was lesbian dramatization? The house had a reputation. Every queer woman in the city seemed to have a fond memory of it. According to Trinket's rough count, at least eighty-six people had had sex in their bathroom.

There used to be at least a dozen legendary queer houses in the neighbourhood. These veteran rentals were the sight of many a whiskey-and-poker game and spin-the-bottle party. They housed burlesque troupe rehearsals and taiko drum practises and knitting circles. They served as art studios and grassroots soup kitchens and queer dungeons. Most were owned by Italian or Greek, sometimes by Chinese landlords, who had left East Van for the suburbs and paid little attention to what happened on or around their rental properties.

But when real estate rose so high that even a dilapidated wartime bungalow was worth more than half a million, these landlords paid attention. One by one the houses wound up with for-sale signs spiked into their overgrown front yards. These signs may as have well been tombstones; they marked the death of another queer sanctuary. The tenants were forced to split up and move further east, or north, or wherever rent was cheap. Queer neighbourhoods disbanded.

"This is what we're going to do, Mommy," Trinket had told Zoya when they received their eviction notice. "We're going to fucking chain ourselves to the front porch. Us and all our friends, and all our friends' friends, and, hell, we'll invite any homo with a length of chain who wants to stand up to the yuppies that keep buying up East Van."

But their last night had arrived without a gathering of protesters. Trinket grew sad just thinking about the new owners who would arrive the next morning, probably armed with colour swatches and nonfat macchiatos in hand. She leaned up against the outside wall, not caring about the rough glass stucco against her bare skin. "Fuck it," she said after a moment of feeling sorry for herself, "I'm going down to the fucking basement."

The basement door creaked predictably as Trinket pushed it open. The first step groaned under her foot. And her fingers brushed against something sticky and delicate—probably a cob-web—as she searched for the railing. Light came flickering in from under the rim of the blindfold, filling the room with enough warmth to give Trinket courage. Her plan was simple: curl up as small as she could get underneath the last step and wait to be found. It was a good hiding spot, one that Zoya wouldn't expect her to choose willingly. But before she reached the bottom of the stairs she heard footsteps coming quickly down behind her.

"Not fair. That couldn't have been ten minutes," Trinket whined. Zoya responded by slamming the basement door, and Trinket understood perfectly that Zoya wasn't playing by any-one's rules but her own. The door screeched open and slammed a second time, then opened again. "You've got me good and scared, Mommy," Trinket said, backing away from the stair-case. Something scraped along the stairwell. Maybe Zoya's fingernails, or maybe something sharper? The sound instantly unnerved Trinket. "Really scared," she confirmed. The warm, candle-lit atmosphere shifted to heavy darkness. The sound came again from the other side of the basement. And again a few feet from where Trinket stood. "What's that you've got for me, Mommy?"

Zoya didn't answer. The cruel echo of metallic scrapes and heavy shuffles continued; the sound seemed to literally bounce from one end of the room to the next. Trinket had seen Zoya move fast before, even in heels, but there in the darkened base-ment she had Trinket spinning in blind circles. A couple of times the noises got so close that Trinket let out a high, uncensored scream, punctuating the long, silent gaps when Trinket could hear only the sound of her own frantic panting. She grew des-perate for one of Zoya's orders: *kneel, beg, swallow* ... anything but unidentifiable scraping. Several agonizing minutes of this had Trinket crying. Her tears soaked into the blindfold, and the small sliver of sight under the edge of the blindfold blurred. Trinket bit her lip to keep her from using her safe word.

Gradually the scraping turned into loud rattling, like a chandelier or a stack of wine glasses being shaken. "What the hell is that?" Trinket shouted, her voice stripped of any cuteness. She dropped to a squat and frantically tried to pry the blindfold off with her knees. This is when Zoya made her move.

A feather-soft touch grazed Trinket just behind her left ear. Fingers tangled in her hair and yanked her down toward the concrete floor. Her bound ankles were raised high, forcing Trinket onto her back and lifting her ass several inches off the floor. This time Trinket kicked and struggled, but her ankle bondage barely moved. It was as if she'd been strung up—but from what? Zoya must have installed some strong hook in the basement ceiling beams without her knowing. Trinket gave up the struggle. Legs dangling, arms trapped behind her back, she was more helpless than an upside-down crab.

Something slid inside her so deeply her leg muscles spasmed. No warmup strokes or licks, just sharp and immediate penetration. An icy current shot through Trinket's body. For a brief moment, she tried to grasp what was fucking her: magnetic dildo, electric-pulse vibrator, trickling garden hose? Whatever it was, it took her completely. Before long her guessing gave way to mindless sensation. Her skin tingled with goose bumps and went numb. Her muscles relaxed. She could hardly utter the word "yes." Her own moaning felt as if it was being ripped out of her mouth; a moment later she was mute. Hallucinations crept in behind the blindfold: strange eyes peering back at her, strange hands reaching out. Then darkness. Pussy juice dripped down her ass crack, oddly chilly, but oozing nonetheless down to the floor where a slippery pool formed beneath her. Zoya was fucking her cold and stupid. It was the only thing Trinket knew or felt—that something unknown and all-consuming was moving in and out of her. More and more of the tangible world slid away with each thrust.

Despite the fact that the Gambinis had very little family in Vancouver, Guido gave Biba a proper Southern Italian funeral. Teary-eyed, he folded one of her Sunday dresses, tucked it into his jacket next to his heart, and took it to Woodward's, where a sympathetic sales girl helped him pick out a burial outfit. The chosen blouse was printed with pink tea roses, though Biba never wore pink. "I bet she'd like this one," the sales girl assured Guido as she led him to the cash register.

Guido ordered too much food from the delicatessen and crowded the table with their best ceramics and silverware. He could have filled a mixing bowl with the olives alone. Calla lily and chrysanthemum wreaths blanketed every available flat surface in the house. All the clocks were stopped at the time of Biba's death. The open casket was laid in the living room, beside which Guido stood for hours as his neighbours arrived to pay their respects. The wives kissed Guido's cheeks. The husbands shook their heads and stared at the floor. By mid-day Biba's coffin was filled with chocolates, candles and matches, rosewater, tiny bottles of lemon liqueurs, and other comfort items for the soul.

The Giampolo girl from across the street, not really a girl anymore but still living with her parents, brought a sugar-soaked fig wrapped in real lace. Guido watched, flabbergasted, as the girl eased the fig into Biba's lifeless hand then rushed away without so much as a consoling handshake.

At dusk she reappeared in Guido's living room and shuffled up to him holding a wicker crate in her arms. Guido took his hands out of his trouser pockets, ready to accept what he thought was a care package sent by the girl's elderly parents. He'd heard that the Giampolos made the best lemon ricotta cookies around. But the girl surprised him by saying, "I hope you don't mind, I've collected just a little of Biba's canning. Only tomatoes and pears, nothing special. The tuna in oil I wouldn't dream of touching, unless you yourself didn't want it. As you know, I spent a lot of time helping Biba in the garden."

Guido didn't know. He'd barely exchanged greetings with the young woman standing before him. The only reason he remembered her name was because she was named after the island of Capri—a place Guido had said he would one day take Biba for the honeymoon they never got to have as newlyweds. In fact, it was money from the Capri holiday savings fund that largely paid for Biba's funeral. The girl was a blight based on her name alone. And who gave her permission to sneak down to the basement? Her cheeks were heavily stained in salt from tears. *Has she never heard of a handkerchief?* Guido wondered. *Why should she cry? Am I crying?—No.* So although the girl's shoulders were hunched in a way that told Guido she was carrying more than just a few jars, Guido's gut told him not to get into conversation with her as he was about to wrap up his wife's wake. He threw his hands up at her. "*Che me ne fotto?*" he said. "What do I care?"

As her internal clock counted down the minutes, Zoya itemized the contents of her briefcase: scissors, self-warming lubricant, extra rope, a large vinyl hand-held dildo shaped like a police baton, and a flannel drop sheet.

The flannel was plagued by stains of every imaginable fluid: bodily, edible, and otherwise. Recently, Trinket had taken up using the spotted sheet as a security blanket and dragged it around the house like a toddler. Zoya couldn't help but be annoyed that Trinket developed this filthy, shameful habit all on her on her own. What next—she'd start licking her own boots? *This is this flannel's last night*, Zoya decided. It would be left by the front door as a welcome mat for the new owners, right after she ordered Trinket to pee on it. She wanted to do worse. Maybe in her younger years she'd have kicked a couple of holes in the drywall or spray-painted obscenities on the floor. Instead she found herself casting the evil eye on the blanket. A swift moment later she asked that the curse be undone—better not to mess with fate. A moment after that she scolded herself for her unwanted superstitions. Restless, she slung the dildo baton over her shoulder and started toward the main floor. If she crept quietly, perhaps she'd catch Trinket floundering in an empty closet.

She heard moaning before she reached the living room and pictured Trinket bent like a bow so that she could pleasure herself with her tied hands. "She better not be …" Zoya growled.

Sure enough, as she made her way to the basement door, there was Trinket with her legs in the air at the bottom of the stairs. "Get up," she barked. Trinket didn't move. Zoya dropped the flannel sheet and bundle of sex toys to the floor; a gesture that indicated she was not playing. "You'll be sorry if I have to come down there." Zoya waited no more than ten seconds, then flicked on the dingy basement light and started down the stairs.

Her temper turned to worry with each descending step. Midway down the basement stairs she stopped short. Trinket wasn't loose from the bondage. She wasn't circling her clit with her bratty fingers. Her moaning was off. Listening closer, Trinket was gagging; foamy drool leaked out of the left corner of her mouth. Her arms were pinned under her and her slender neck was twisted like an arbutus branch.

Zoya—who practically insisted on being well-grounded and in control of any situation—froze mid-stairs wondering what to do. *The move has made her crazy. Crap, I really liked having a sane girlfriend.* She tried to remember what to do when someone loses their mind. Speak in a slow calm voice? Splash their face with water? Restrain them—

"Trinket," Zoya said with unwanted panic in her voice. "Trinket, I'm going to come, slowly, down the stairs, now. Here I come." Zoya narrated her careful journey, desperately hoping to catch Trinket's attention. Trinket made no motion of recognition. With each step closer Zoya noticed something strange.

Trinket's body looked depressed in a way that neither bondage nor gravity could account for, like an unseen weight was on her. Her tiny breasts bounced. Her ass cheeks twitched as if they were being hit.

"Please, Trin, please snap out of it," Zoya stood before Trinket and pleaded.

"Please don't be having a seizure," she begged as she knelt down to touch her girlfriend.

"Please be okay," she repeated over and over as she urgently undid the bondage around Trinket's ankles. How long had her feet been suspended above her like that? Her feet hadn't gone cold, at least. Her flesh wasn't bluish at all, not even the tips of her toes. By all accounts she looked like she still had good circulation, but Trinket did nothing to indicate she felt Zoya's hands. The ropes refused to undo as quickly as Zoya wanted; it was enough time for Zoya to begin blaming herself, *What have I done?* and *Why do I have to play this way?* She desperately began to repent, *I promise to be a good, normal woman if you just let Trinket be okay.* Zoya didn't even know whose forgiveness she was asking for exactly. Nonetheless, before Trinket was fully untied she'd agreed to give up every last perverted notion her mind was capable of.

"Shake out your limbs," Zoya finally said. "You're loose now, Trinket." She knelt beside Trinket's head for just a second to brace for the worst. Saying one last prayer to no particular deity, Zoya reached for the blindfold. She pulled off the satiny fabric with trepidation. Trinket's eyes were full white, filmy and blood-shot; it startled Zoya so much that she shook her. She grabbed Trinket by the face and shook her as though her eyes were marbles in a children's game that could be manoeuvred back into place.

Miraculously it worked. Trinket's left eye rolled down followed by her right. And with her eyes came vision, new vision for both of them. The room lit up with a strange haze that made

Zoya squint. There was the deafening noise of glass smashing; shards spun from out of nowhere, turning in a ghostly storm around them. Something dark and horrible and inhuman was mounted on top of Trinket. Zoya's stomach flipped and turned to rot as she realized the thing had a face and hair and hands— one of which was sunk deeply between Trinket's legs.

When Zoya screamed it plunged its other hand inside her mouth and Zoya felt it burn down her throat like hot whiskey. She tried and failed to bite her way loose. Her jaw was paralyzed. The thing jerked her head side to side. It had them both like hand puppets. A ribbon of slimy drool rolled down Zoya's chin. Trinket's thighs glistened with sticky wet come, and also with swatches of crusty, egg-white film, evidence that she had orgasmed more than once. Zoya watched feebly until she could no longer stand it.

With all the fire in her gut she screamed "No!" The word came choking up. "Get off of her!" The thing turned lighter, like smoke, and seemed to pause to listen. Trinket's body went limp for a moment. She cried Zoya's name and Zoya shouted, "Run!"

Their legs moved without thought. Zoya's high heels pounded up the basement steps. Trinket's bare feet paddled across the kitchen floor. Before they knew it they had crossed the front yard, leapt over the wooden fence, and locked themselves inside Zoya's car.

Zoya counted to ten out loud, and then from ten down to zero, and repeated it as she drove shakily down the street, shouldering the curb a few times. Trinket counted with her, although she wouldn't lift her head from the fetal position. At least if Zoya crashed into something, Trinket was already prepared for impact.

Her driving steadied by the time they hit the highway. The road was theirs at this hour. A half moon hung low on the horizon. In a few hours there would be daylight. Zoya started planning: bank machine; coffee and a bagel at Tim Hortons at six a.m.; call Visa when they open to tell them, "No, my credit card wasn't stolen. Yes, I did mean to take out a $2,000 cash advance"; call Dad and beg him to keep Banjo for the week; send the office an email saying, "I'll be taking bereavement leave"; and, finally, turn off my Blackberry. After that Zoya had no set agenda.

"I think it was a lady ghost," Trinket said as she unfurled into an upright position. She yawned and propped her feet onto the dashboard. Zoya relaxed back into the driver's seat a little more. The sight of her girlfriend sprawled out naked greatly reassured her. Maybe as a joke, Zoya'd buy her a children's Tim Hortons T-shirt. Maybe when the roadside tourist shops opened she'd get them matching tacky tracksuits. It would be days, at least, before they were home and could get at their own clothes.

"I heard her saying a woman's name, Kathy ... Katie ... something," said Trinket. "Maybe that was her name. Did you hear it?"

"If I can't find a drive-through, I'm going to have to go into Tim Hortons wearing my corset."

"Don't change the subject, Zoya," Trinket said. It was true, Zoya was avoiding any talk about the thing, the ghost.

"No, I only heard the gurgling noises you were making. I thought you were choking."

"Hmm. Did you see her?"

"I wish I hadn't," said Zoya. She fidgeted with her seat belt. "It will take me a while before I get the image of that monster out of my head."

"Monster? Really? You didn't see a young woman?"

Zoya shook her head and clenched her jaw.

"I always knew there was a ghost in the basement," Trinket said. "Lots of people knew."

"Oh, Trin, you would have believed the entire crew of the Titanic was haunting the house if that was the gossip."

"I believe what I saw. We both saw it." Trinket turned to Zoya, waiting for her to confirm her statement. Zoya's resistance to talking about it was beginning to frustrate her. "I wonder why she didn't come out until now?" Trinket said, probing for a response. Zoya shrugged, her eyes fixed on the road.

"Maybe she knew it was her last call for hot dyke action."

"Trinket!" Zoya gasped.

Trinket let out a little giggle. She had Zoya's attention now. "Aren't you the least bit curious about what just happened to us?" she asked.

"Did she hurt you?" It was the only detail Zoya really cared to know.

"No," said Trinket. "I don't think so."

Zoya took Trinket's hand in hers. She rubbed Trinket's wrist where she'd tightened the ropes. "Did I hurt you?" she asked.

Trinket looked at Zoya with her mascara-smudged eyes. "Never," she said and smiled assuredly. "You never do."

Capri Giampolo, seventy-one years old, the neighbourhood spinster as she had been know by her generation, sat in the dark staring out the front window.

For her entire life, the house on Sixth Avenue were she lived had remained exactly the same. A reproduction of Gainsborough's Blue Boy hung above the mantle. Gold brocade sofa set. A bowl of dusty glass grapes in the centre of the dining room table. This was the backdrop to her silence and loneliness. She prayed that her parents, may they rest in peace, would forgive her for selling their house and giving away whatever the Goodwill agreed to take.

She had packed according to her own heart: "Does this make me happy?" she asked herself about every last possession. "Not happy enough to hold on to." Before the week was done, she'd managed to condense the entire split-level bungalow into the living room. The movers were due at eleven the next morning.

It took forever to convince Guido, *that old coot*, to sell. *And what was he going to do with the money now?* Capri fumed. He was eighty and arthritic and had no grandchildren. Though Guido didn't matter much to Capri; he never had. She already had possession of the keys. The deeds were all signed. The tenants had certainly left—and made quite a spectacle of it. Through her window she had watched them peel away in their car, screaming, like heathen banshees in the night. Normally Capri would have clicked her tongue disapprovingly at the sight, but she took the girls' mad flight as a sign, another one of Biba's many signs.

In just a few more hours it would be eight a.m. on July 1, 2006, and the house across the street that Capri had always wanted to live in would finally be hers. She was moving in with her one true love.

Not long after Biba's funeral, Capri began to notice small, yet decidedly odd events at the Gambini house. The lights would flicker. The door would unlatch by itself and swing open. On more than one occasion Capri walked past and swore she saw Biba peeking through the basement window at her, still waving her secret wave like she did when she was alive. And every spring all of the cherry blossom petals from the tree in front of Biba's house blew into, and only into, Capri's front yard.

It took years, decades, for Capri to believe. She waved these strange signs away as grief-induced hallucinations, or perhaps God's way of punishing her for her sins. But she was an old woman now, and reason and religion had little value left in her life. In fact most everything important to her had changed or moved on.

But the house was still there, and she was sure that Biba's presence remained inside. She was too excited to sleep; all night she had been beckoning her spirit to wake up, whispering to it from her window, "Rise, Biba, rise, I'm coming. I'm coming to you soon." Capri saw the wild light flickering in Biba's basement window and knew her incantation had worked.

And in the basement was Biba's canning, which Capri had saved from time. She held a jar of apricots in her weathered hands. For nearly fifty years she had babied this jar. Kept it cool, kept it from denting or bulging. At dawn Capri decided to greet the day with some of Biba's long-awaited fruit. The preserved apricots sighed as she pried the lid off. She raised the jar to her lips to sip the nectar. It tasted as sweet as the day she and Biba canned it. Capri remembered the taste of sugar straight from Biba's fingertips. She raised the jar in the direction of her new home and toasted, "*Salute, amora mia.* To us."

Fear of Dying to the Wrong Song

Amanda Lamarche

There is no such thing as slowing this down.
You are on your way to a day you planned
to spend alone. You now know only that
you are alive in the taxicab, seconds before it pours
itself around a pole. You hear the prayer
of the driver, a woman yelling through the inch
of your opened window, and then neither. Just
the song coming softly through the system.
And it is not the kind of song that makes you
hang your head in your hands, give up, not
the gravelled voice of a poisoned smoker
about to outlive you, or a hymn that lets
you go. It is the soundtrack of a hand
on your back, the way your mother hums
when she picks up the telephone. You think
of it as you clamour to the curb, as you
prop yourself against the collapsed salt box.
You can still hear the strings. Kissed
on the face by a leaf, you cannot bother
to remove it. You know when the song
picks up. You picture the cello being
crushed between the knees, the pianist

pedalling in coal black shoes, the femur
of the flute in the flautist's lap, shining, geared.
There is the taste of that steel on your lips. You
inhale to make any sort of sound. You almost
place your mouth there and breathe.

AUTHOR BIOGRAPHIES

Mette Bach is a freelance writer who contributes to the *Advocate*, the *Globe and Mail*, *Xtra! West,* and *Vancouver Magazine*. She wrote the syndicated column "Not That Kind of Girl" for nearly four years, sharing her queer adventures with the red states. Now she writes a column called "From Queer To Eternity" for *Xtra! West*. One of her short stories, "Unfriendly," is in the Lambda Award-winning anthology *First Person Queer* (Arsenal Pulp Press, 2007). She's currently working on a book about femme identity and finishing an MFA in Creative Writing at the University of British Columbia.

Elizabeth Bachinsky is the author of *Curio: Grotesques and Satires from the Electronic Age* (BookThug, 2005) and *Home of Sudden Service* (Nightwood, 2006), which was nominated for a Governor General's Award for Poetry. Her third collection, *Strange Ritual,* will appear from Nightwood Editions (2009). She lives in Vancouver, BC.

Kestrel Barnes is a butch dyke single parent of five who lives with her family on unceded Coast Salish territory in Vancouver, BC. "Shark" is dedicated to Kestrel's wife, Sally Diana Rowe (1957–1990).

Kristyn Dunnion, a.k.a. Miss Kitty Galore, is a wig-wearing party on wheels. She is the author of *Missing Matthew* (Red Deer Press, 2003), a quirky mystery for rebels of all ages, *Mosh Pit* (Red Deer Press, 2004), a queer punkrawk teen novel, and *Big Big Sky* (Red Deer Press, 2008), a speculative novel about female assassin warriors. Her short stories are widely anthologized. She likes big boots, shaved heads, and loud music. Visit Kristyn at *kristyndunnion.com.*

Aurelia T. Evans graduated in May of 2008 from Trinity University in San Antonio, TX, with a major in English. She was part of her college Sexual Diversity Alliance and Bad Movie Club. Aurelia loves horror movies, Tex-Mex, scented lotions, and philosophical discussions about religion, gender, and sexuality. She is a voluntarily bald woman and proud of it, and she works to raise awareness of trichotillomania.

Amanda Lamarche is a poet and good girl from Gibsons, BC. She has a BA in English from UVic and an MFA in Creative Writing from UBC. Her work has been published in numerous magazines and anthologized in *Breathing Fire 2: Canada's New Poets* (Nightwood, 2004). Her first poetry collection, *The Clichéist*, was published by Nightwood Editions in 2005. Most recently, she has moved to Summerside, PEI, where she works as a medical transcriptionist. She is currently writing her second collection of poetry that is about, among other things, Lucy Maud Montgomery's fictional character Matthew Cuthbert. Although she is not all that queer in the modern sense, on a genetic level she is at least 88 percent oddity.

Nomy Lamm is a writer and musician currently living in San Francisco. She is an advice columnist and section editor for *Make/Shift Magazine* (*makeshiftmag.com*). Her writing has been published in anthologies including *Listen Up: Voices from the Next Feminist Generation* (1995), *Word Warriors: 35 Women Leaders in the Spoken Word Revolution* (2007), and *Working Sex: Sex Workers Write About a Changing Industry* (2007), all from Seal Press. She is currently working on her first novel, *The Best Part Comes After the End.*

Larissa Lai is an Assistant Professor in Canadian Literature in the Department of English at the University of British Columbia. Her first novel, *When Fox Is a Thousand* (Press Gang, 1995; reprinted by Arsenal Pulp Press, 2004), was shortlisted for the Chapters/*Books in Canada* First Novel Award. Her second novel, *Salt Fish Girl* (Thomas Allen Publishers, 2002), was shortlisted for the Sunburst Award, the Tiptree Award, and the City of Calgary W.O. Mitchell Award. In 2004, *West Coast Line* published a special issue focused on her work. *Sybil Unrest*, her collaborative long poem with Rita Wong, was published by Line Books in 2008.

Suki Lee is the author of the short story collection *Sapphic Traffic* (Conundrum, 2003). Her fiction has been featured in such anthologies as *Hot & Bothered 3* and *4* (Arsenal Pulp Press, 2001 and 2003), *The Portable Conundrum* (Conundrum Press, 2006), *With a Rough Tongue: Femmes Write Porn* (Arsenal Pulp Press, 2005), and *Second Person Queer* (Arsenal Pulp Press, 2009). Originally from Montreal, Suki Lee lives in Toronto. *sukilee.com*

Esther Mazakian was born in Israel and shortly after moved to Toronto, where she has lived ever since. Her debut collection of poetry, *All the Lifters*, was published in 2007 by Signature Editions. Her poems have also appeared in several Canadian journals, including the *Malahat Review, PRISM international, Event*, and *Fiddlehead*. Her poetry was an Editor's Choice in *Arc*'s 2002 Arc Poem of the Year Contest and winner of *Prism*'s 2004 Earle Birney Prize for Poetry.

Megan Milks lives in Chicago. She has had fiction published in *DIAGRAM*, *Pocket Myths*, and *Wreckage of Reason: An Anthology of Contemporary XXperimental Prose by Women Writers* (Spuyten Duyvil, 2008). Check out her zine at *mildred-pierce.wordpress.com*.

Michelle Tea is the author of four memoirs, a collection of poetry, and the novel *Rose of No Man's Land* (MacAdam Cage, 2006). She has edited collections, anthologies of personal narratives, working-class and queer-girl writings, and fashion essays. She owns and operates Radar Productions, which runs a monthly reading series and quarterly salon in San Francisco and the all-girl, spoken-word roadshow, Sister Spit: The Next Generation.

Courtney Trouble is a photographer, pornographer, and musician from San Francisco. She is the creator of *NoFauxxx.com*, a queer underground porn site. She is currently teaching herself how to edit video. This is her first piece of published erotica.

Fiona Zedde lives and writes in Atlanta, Georgia, with her partner. She is the author of the novels *Bliss* (2005), *A Taste of Sin* (2006), *Every Dark Desire* (2007), and *Hungry For It* (2008), all from Kensington, as well as the novellas, "Pure Pleasure," "Going Wild," and "Sweat," which appear in the collections *Satisfy Me* (2007), *Satisfy Me Again* (2008), and the soon-to-be-published *Satisfy Me One More Time*, all from Aphrodisia. Find out more at *fionazedde.com*.

About the Editor

Amber Dawn is a writer, filmmaker, and performance artist based in Vancouver. She is the co-editor of *With a Rough Tongue: Femmes Write Porn* (Arsenal Pulp Press, 2005). Her writing has been published in dozens of literary magazines and anthologies, from *Working Sex: Sex Workers Write About a Changing Industry* (Seal Press, 2007) to *Best New Poets 2005* (University of Virginia Press). Currently, she is Director of Programming of the Vancouver Queer Film Festival.